GENE LUEN YANG
& MIKE HOLMES

First Second

New York

First Second

New York

Copyright © 2015 by Humble Comics LLC

Published by First Second
First Second is an imprint of Roaring Brook Press,
a division of Holtzbrinck Publishing Holdings Limited Partnership
175 Fifth Avenue, New York, NY 10010

Cataloging-in-Publication Data is on file at the Library of Congress

Paperback ISBN: 978-1-62672-075-6
Hardcover ISBN: 978-1-62672-276-7

First Second books may be purchased for business or promotional use.
For information on bulk purchases please contact Macmillan Corporate
and Premium Sales Department at (800) 221-7945 x5442 or by email at
specialmarkets@macmillan.com.

FIRST
EDITION

First edition 2015

Book design by Rob Steen

Printed in China by Toppan Leefung Printing Ltd., Dongguan City, Guangdong Province

Paperback: 10
Hardcover: 10 9 8 7 6 5

"It was this wonderful time between magic and so-called rationality."

—Wally Feurzeig, co-creator of the Logo programming language, on the early days of Logo

Chapter

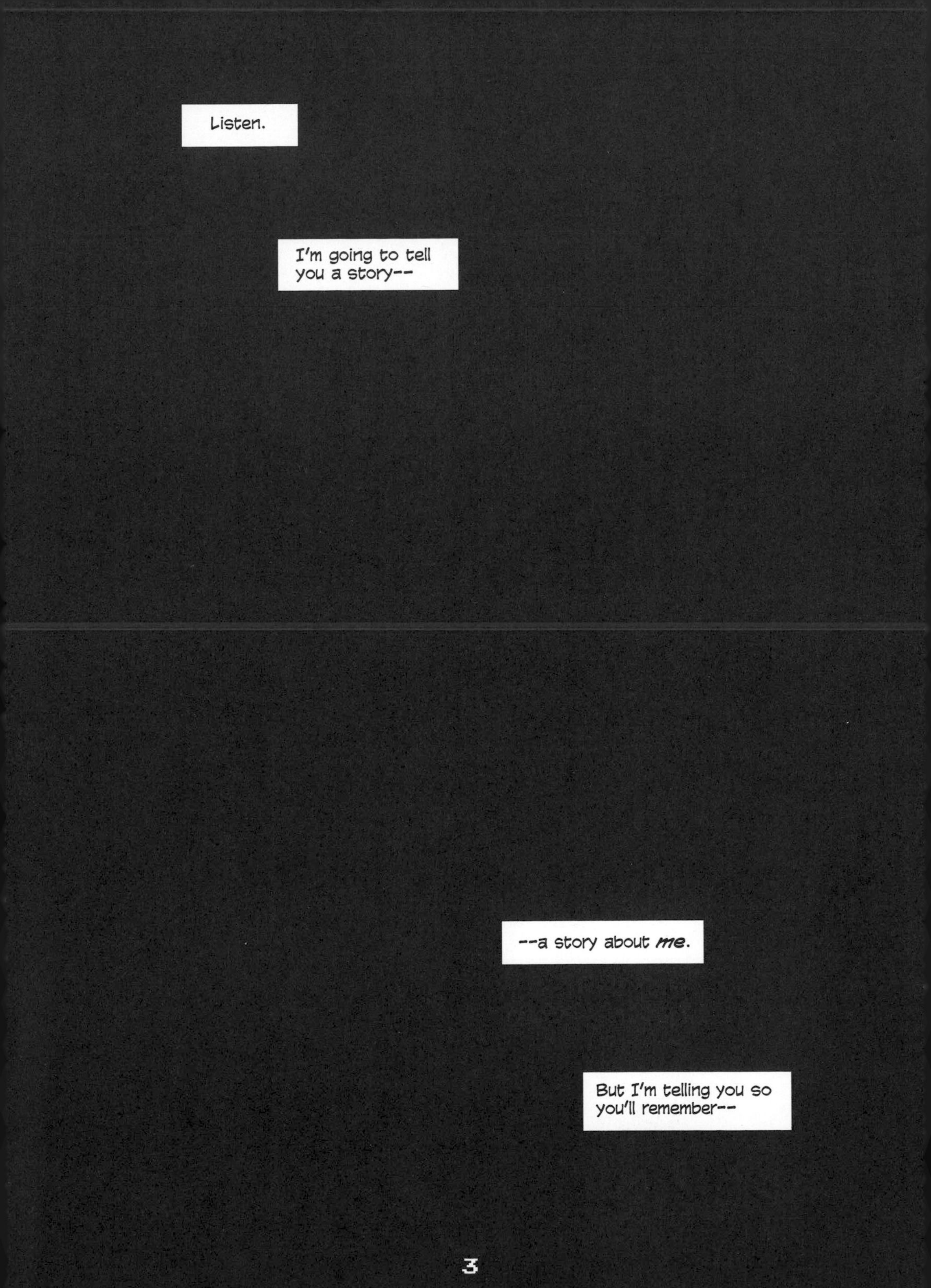
Listen.
I'm going to tell you a story--
--a story about *me*.
But I'm telling you so you'll remember--

--remember about *you*.

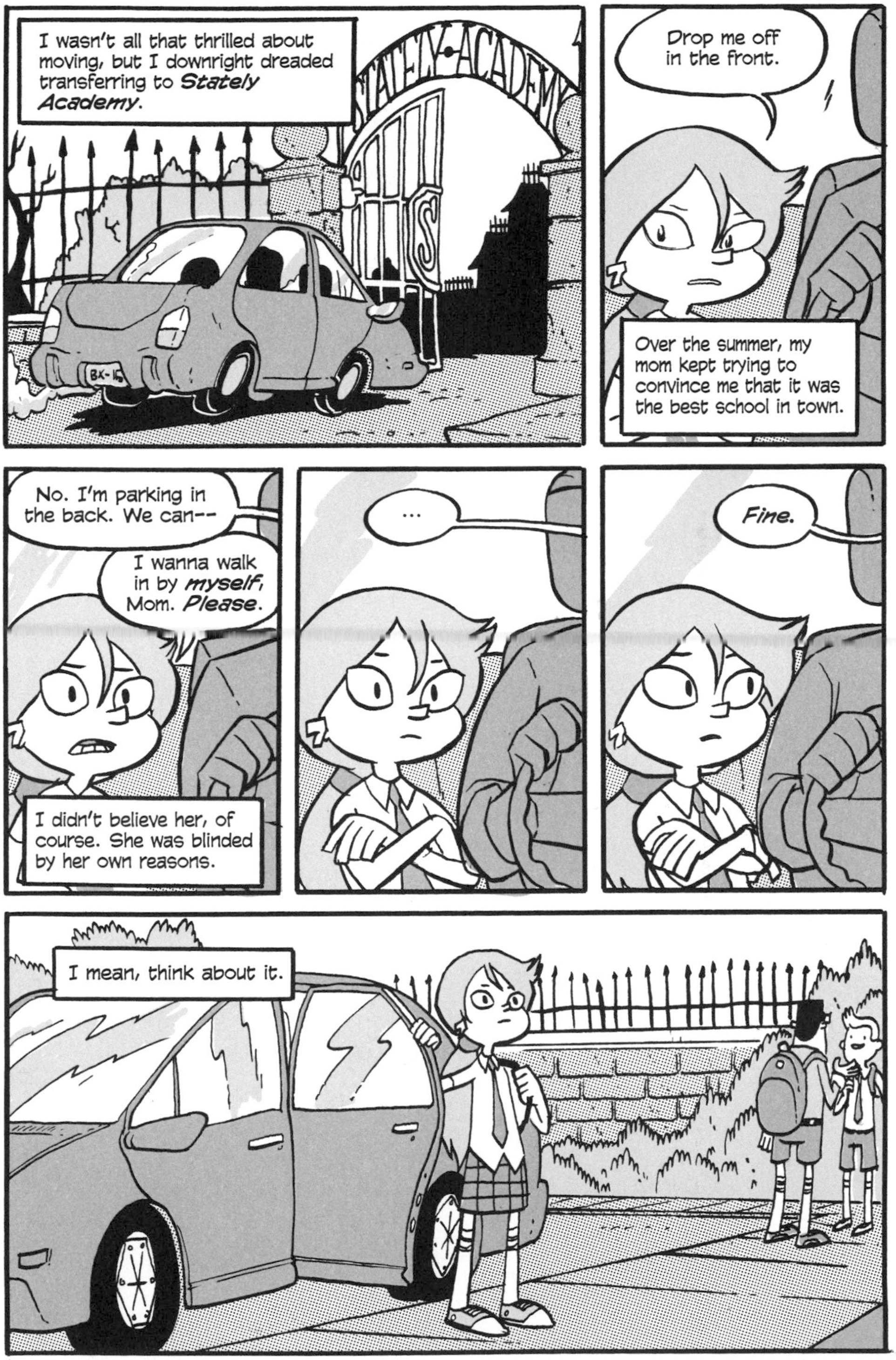
I wasn't all that thrilled about moving, but I downright dreaded transferring to ***Stately Academy***.
STATELY ACADEMY
Drop me off in the front.
Over the summer, my mom kept trying to convince me that it was the best school in town.
No. I'm parking in the back. We can--
I wanna walk in by ***myself***, Mom. ***Please***.
I didn't believe her, of course. She was blinded by her own reasons.
...
Fine.
I mean, think about it.

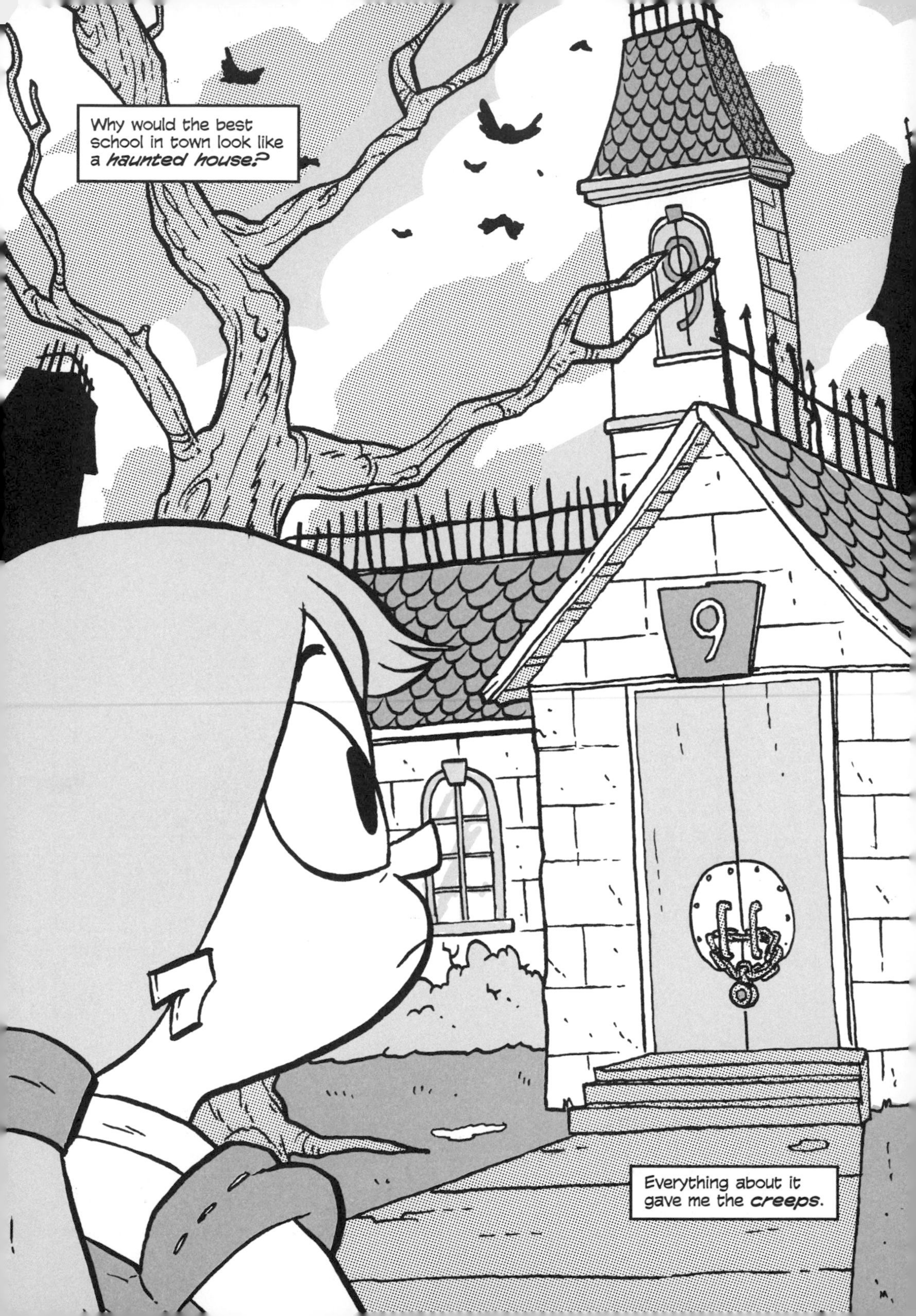
Why would the best school in town look like a *haunted house?*
9
Everything about it gave me the *creeps*.

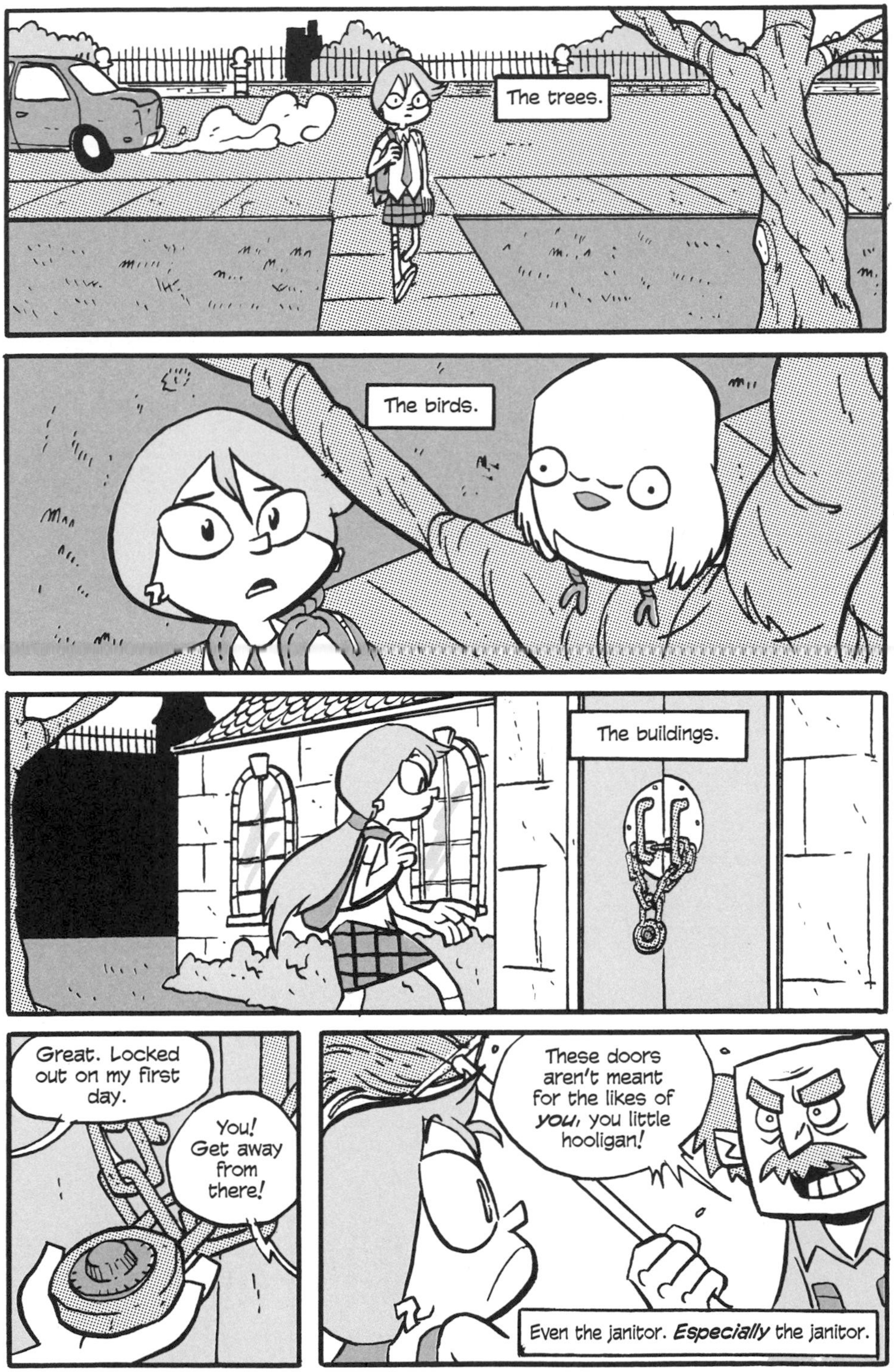
The trees.
The birds.
The buildings.
Great. Locked out on my first day.
You! Get away from there!
These doors aren't meant for the likes of *you*, you little hooligan!
Even the janitor. ***Especially*** the janitor.

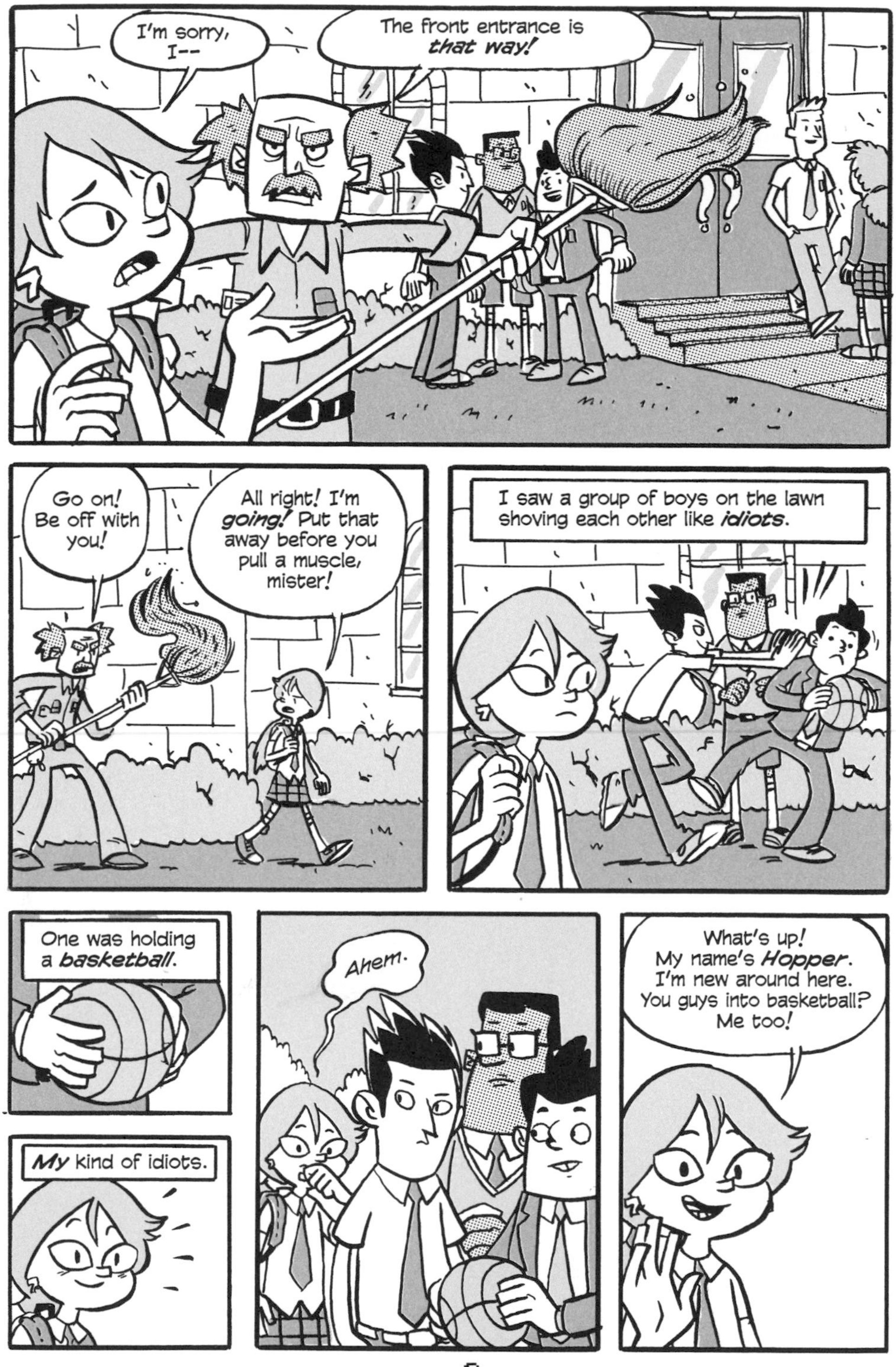

I'm sorry, I--
The front entrance is *that way!*
Go on! Be off with you!
All right! I'm *going!* Put that away before you pull a muscle, mister!
I saw a group of boys on the lawn shoving each other like *idiots*.
One was holding a *basketball*.
My kind of idiots.
Ahem.
What's up! My name's *Hopper*. I'm new around here. You guys into basketball? Me too!

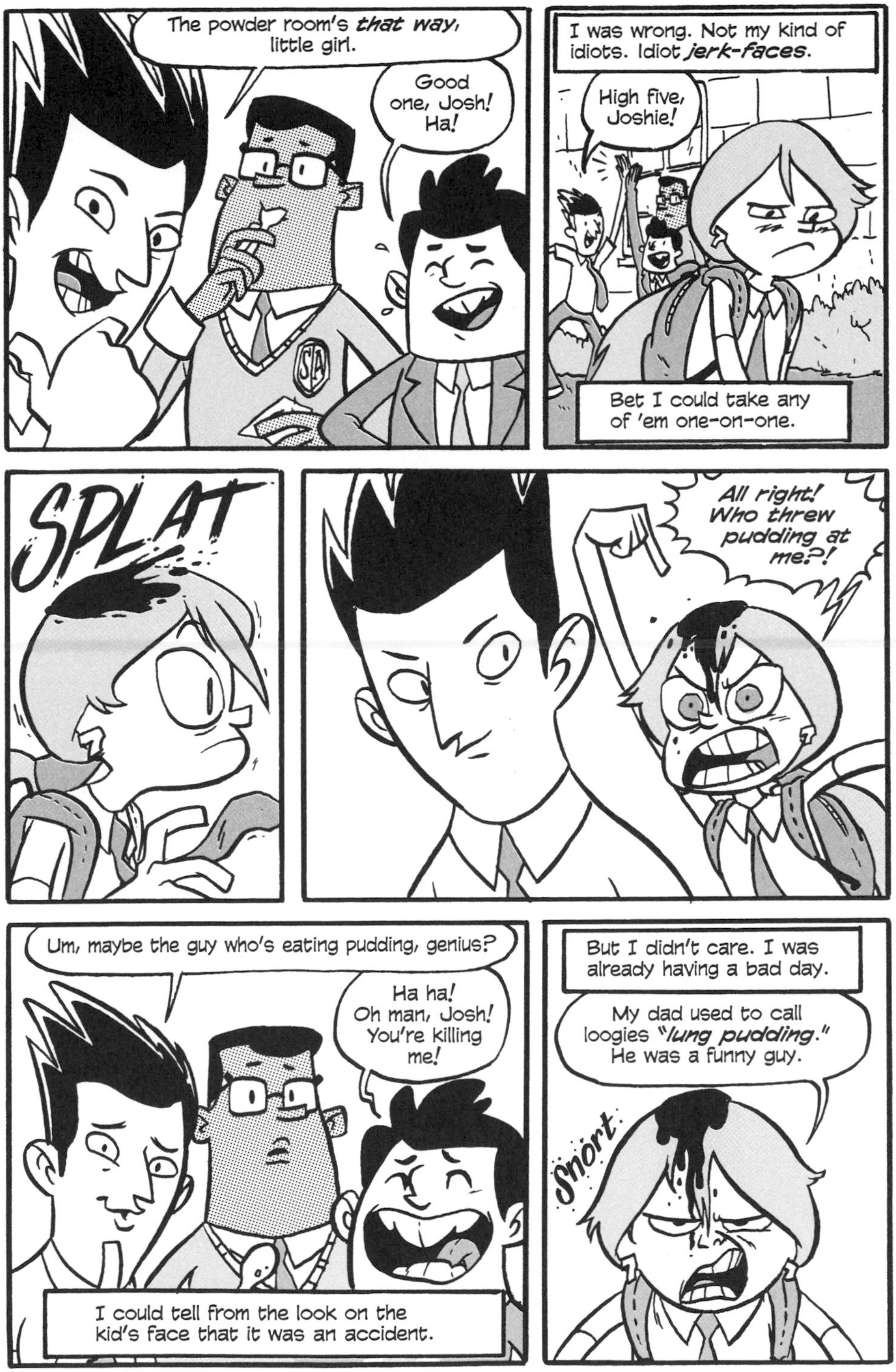

The powder room's *that way,* little girl.
Good one, Josh! Ha!
I was wrong. Not my kind of idiots. Idiot *jerk-faces*.
High five, Joshie!
Bet I could take any of 'em one-on-one.
SPLAT
All right! Who threw pudding at me?!
Um, maybe the guy who's eating pudding, genius?
Ha ha! Oh man, Josh! You're killing me!
I could tell from the look on the kid's face that it was an accident.
But I didn't care. I was already having a bad day.
My dad used to call loogies *"lung pudding."* He was a funny guy.
Snort

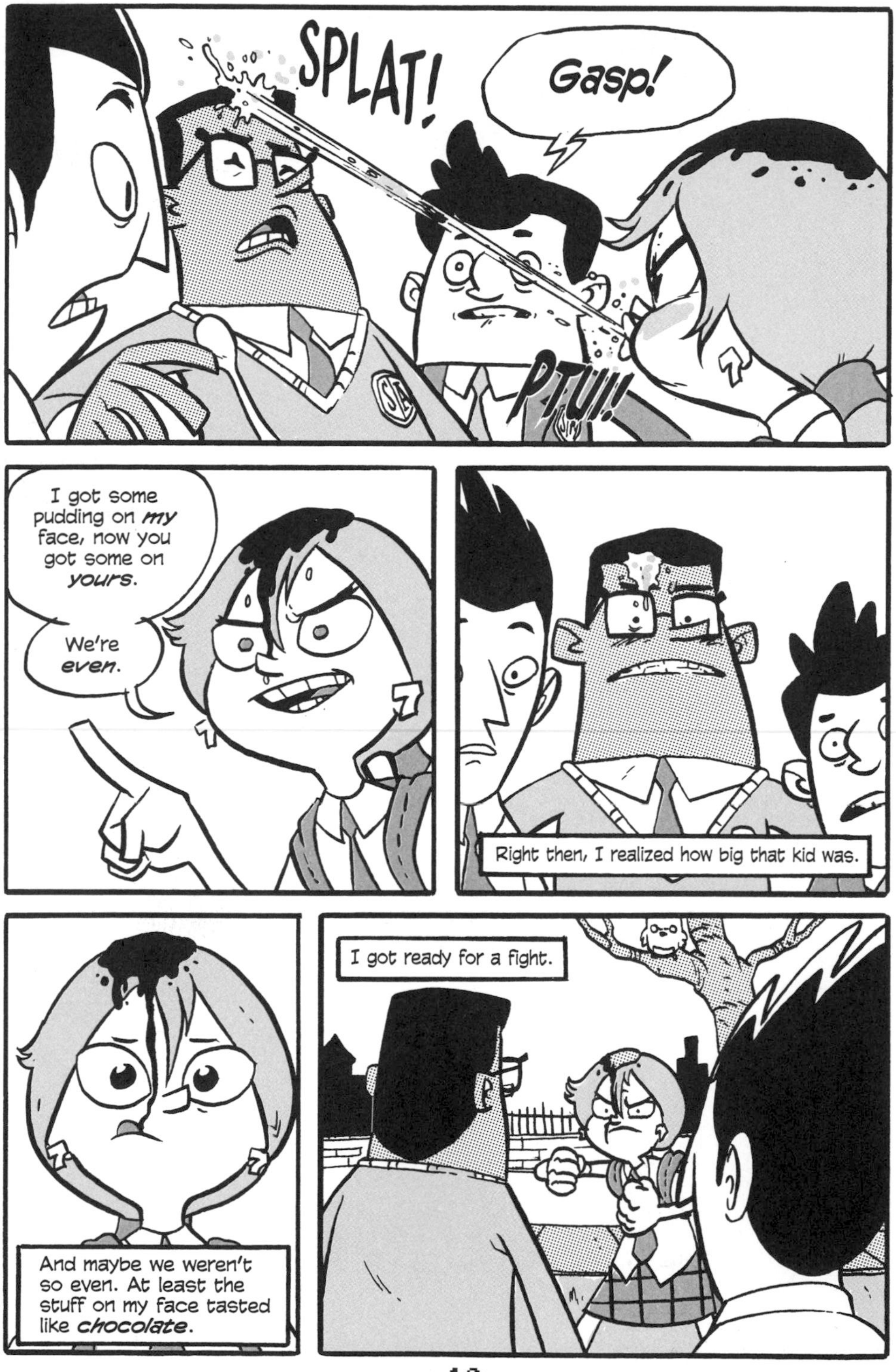
SPLAT!
Gasp!
PTUI!
I got some pudding on *my* face, now you got some on *yours*.
We're *even*.
Right then, I realized how big that kid was.
And maybe we weren't so even. At least the stuff on my face tasted like *chocolate*.
I got ready for a fight.

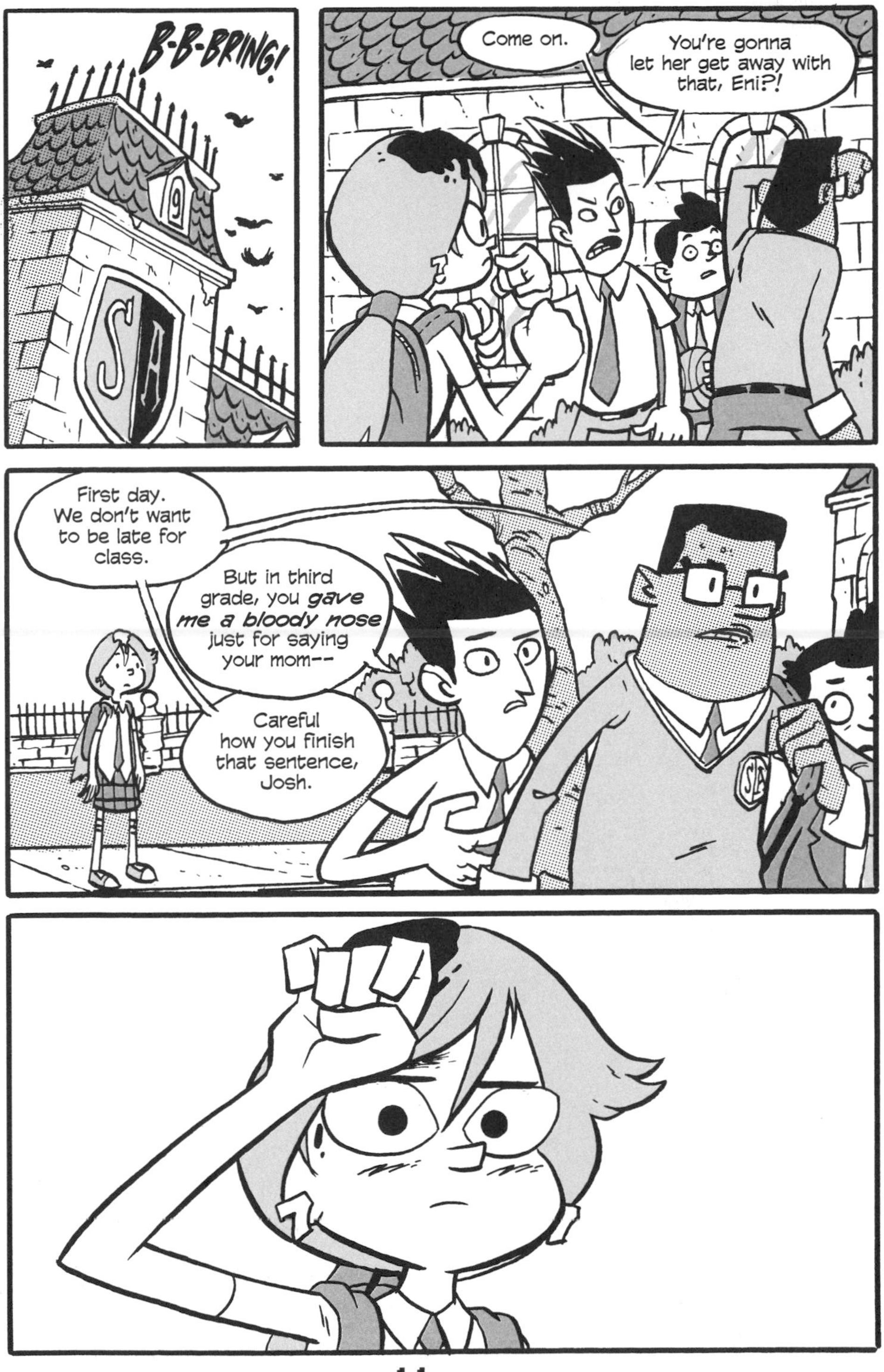

B-B-BRING!
Come on.
You're gonna let her get away with that, Eni?!
First day. We don't want to be late for class.
But in third grade, you ***gave me a bloody nose*** just for saying your mom--
Careful how you finish that sentence, Josh.

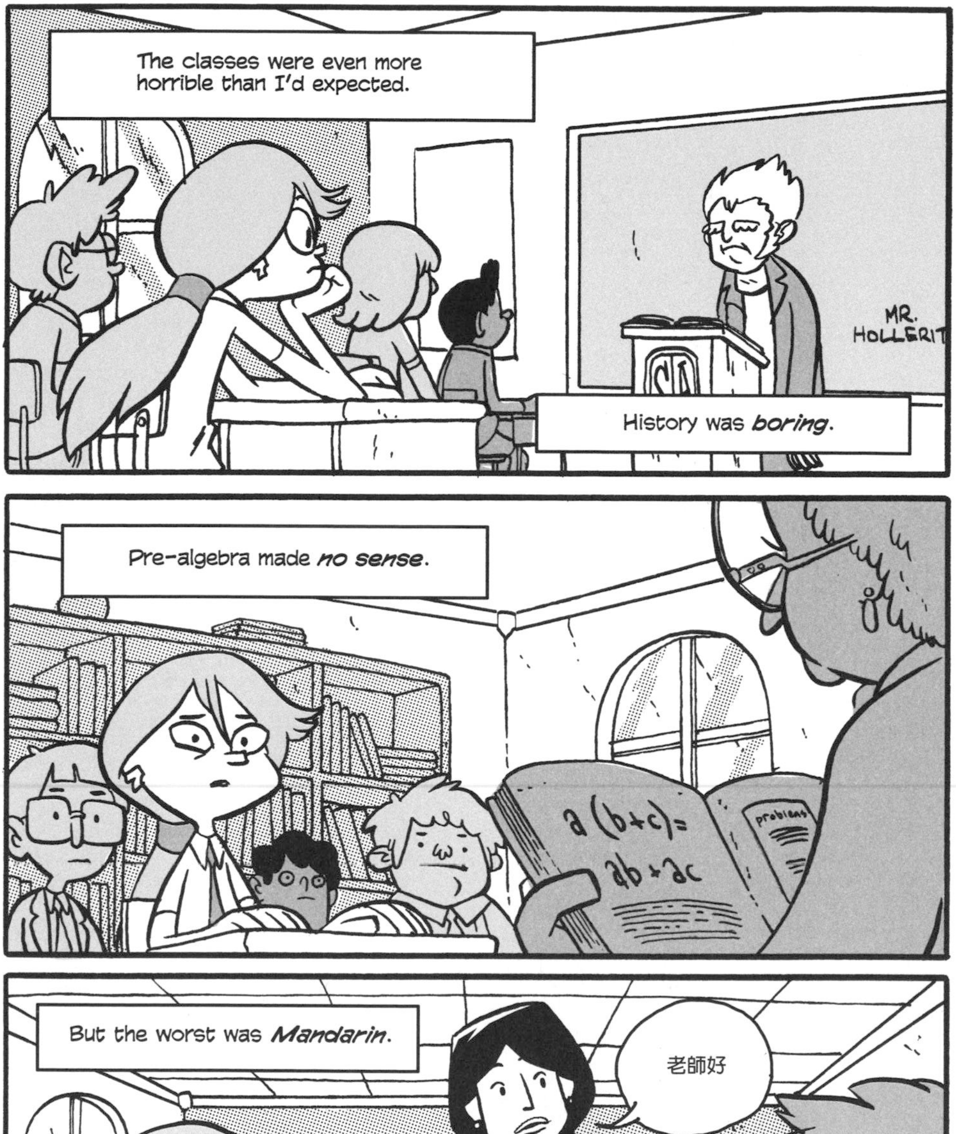
The classes were even more horrible than I'd expected.
MR. HOLLERIT
History was *boring*.
Pre-algebra made *no sense*.
a (b+c)= ab+ac
But the worst was *Mandarin*.
老師好

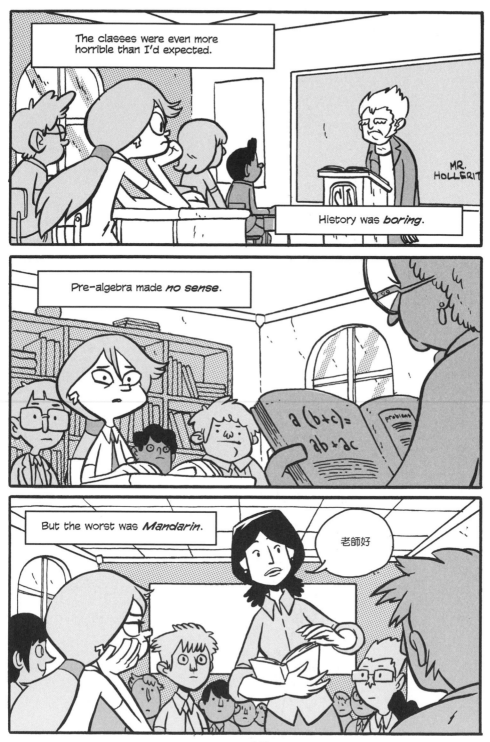

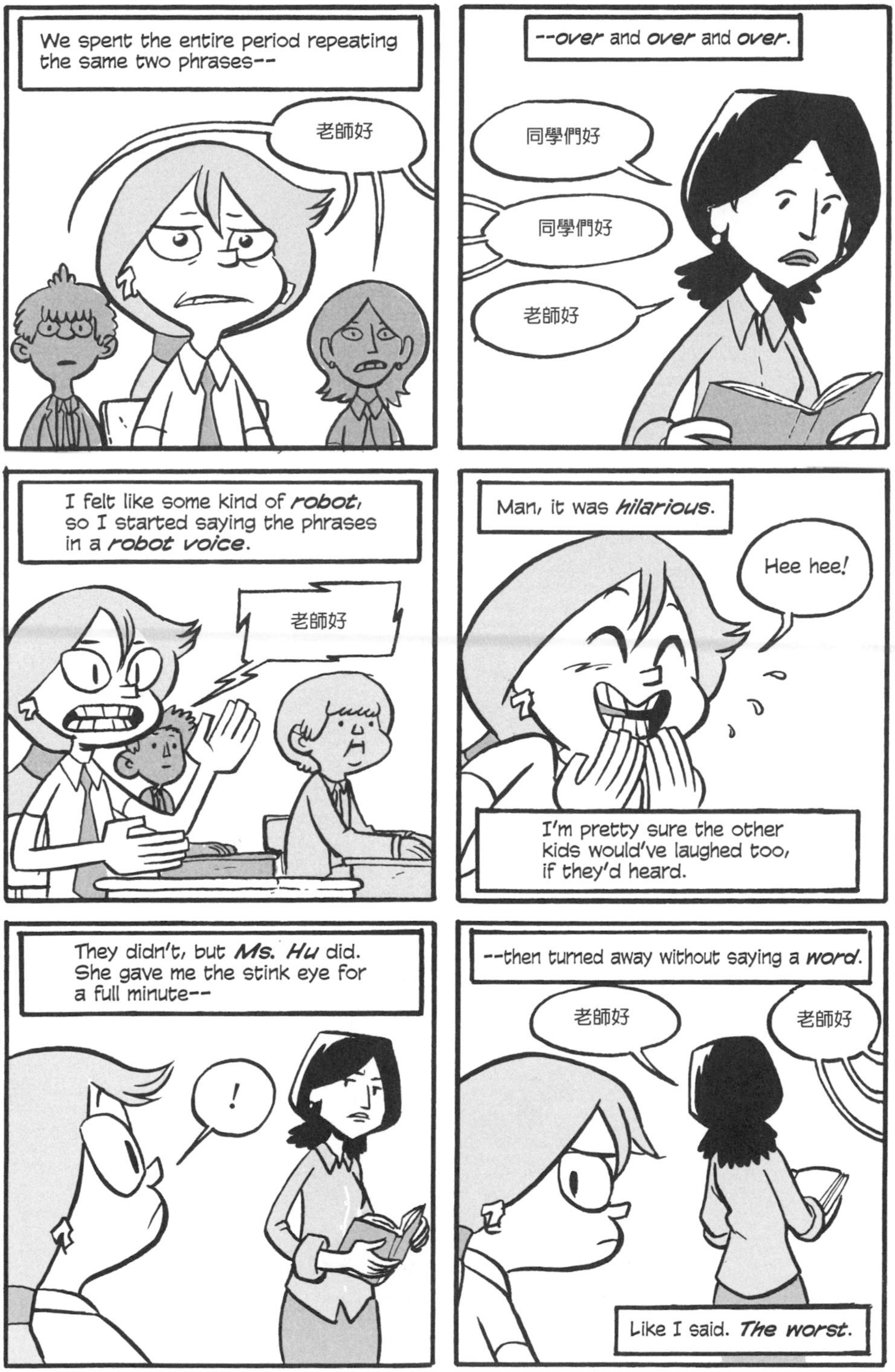
We spent the entire period repeating the same two phrases--
老師好
--*over* and *over* and *over*.
同學們好
同學們好
老師好
I felt like some kind of *robot*, so I started saying the phrases in a *robot voice*.
老師好
Man, it was *hilarious*.
Hee hee!
I'm pretty sure the other kids would've laughed too, if they'd heard.
They didn't, but *Ms. Hu* did. She gave me the stink eye for a full minute--
!
--then turned away without saying a *word*.
老師好
老師好
Like I said. *The worst*.

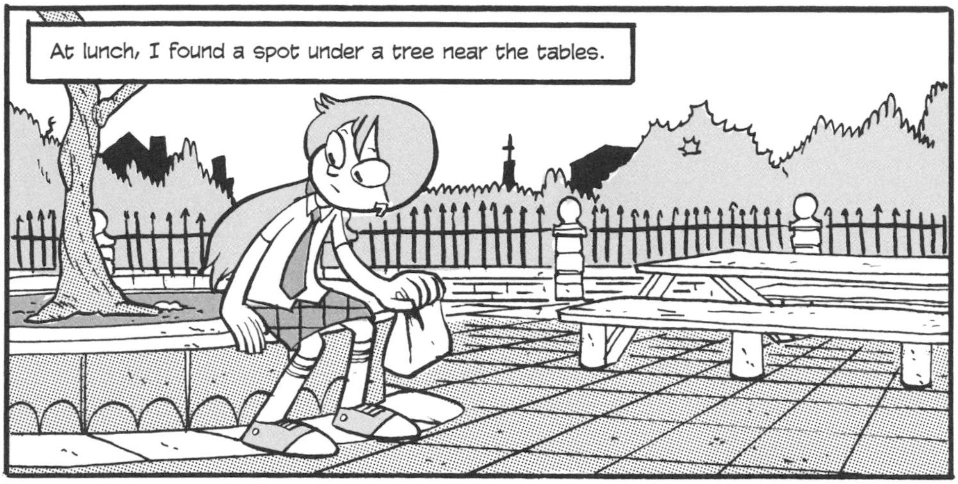
At lunch, I found a spot under a tree near the tables.

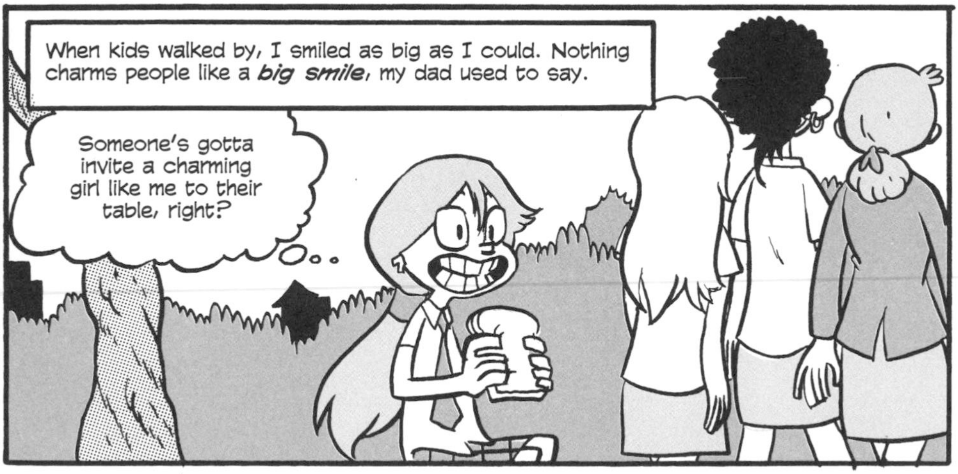
When kids walked by, I smiled as big as I could. Nothing charms people like a *big smile*, my dad used to say.
Someone's gotta invite a charming girl like me to their table, right?

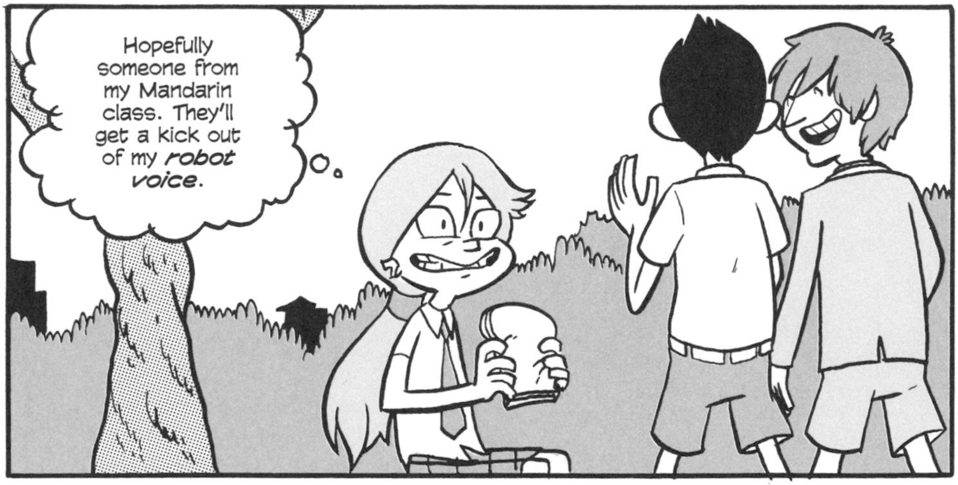
Hopefully someone from my Mandarin class. They'll get a kick out of my *robot voice*.

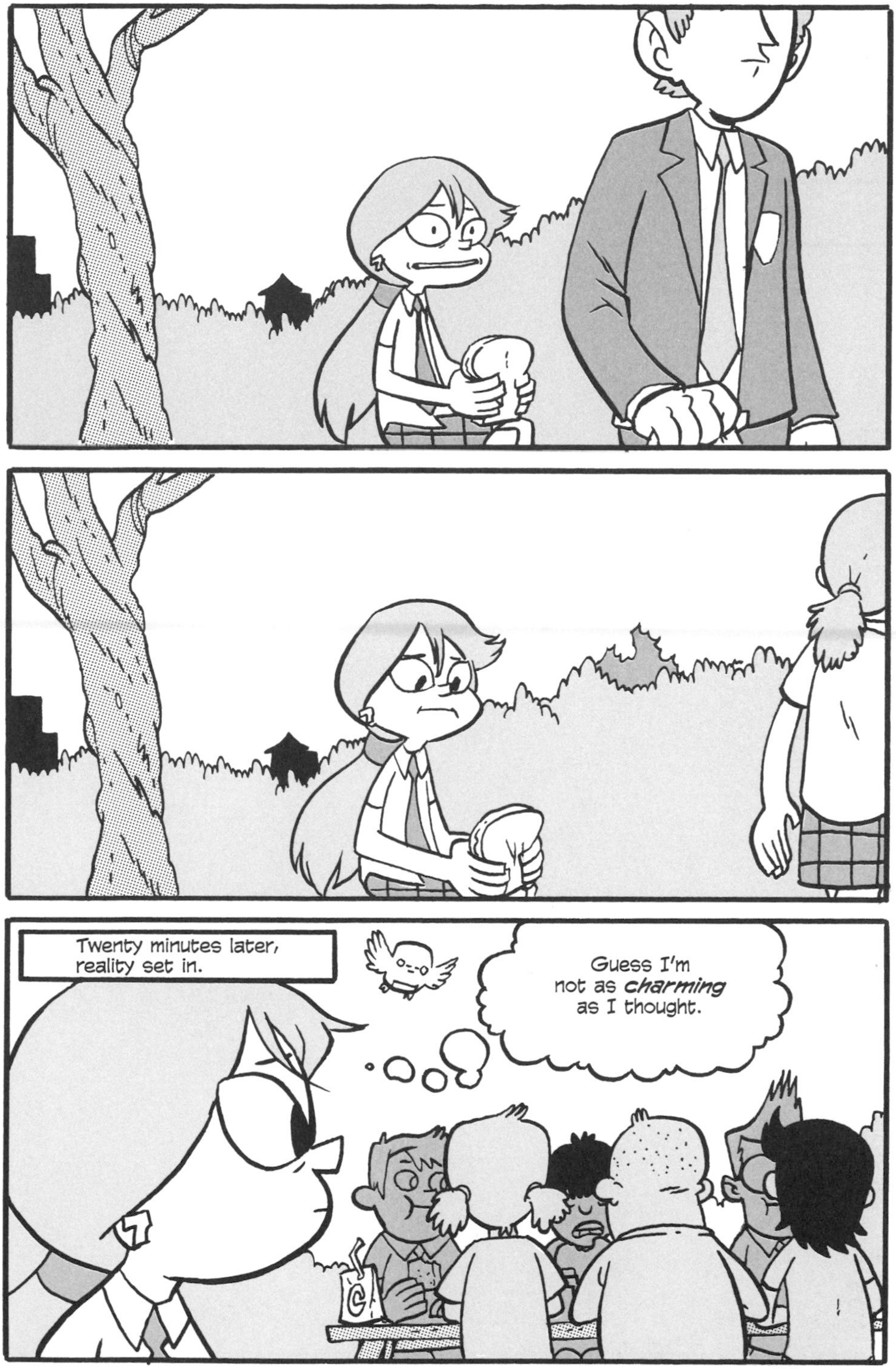
Twenty minutes later, reality set in.
Guess I'm not as *charming* as I thought.

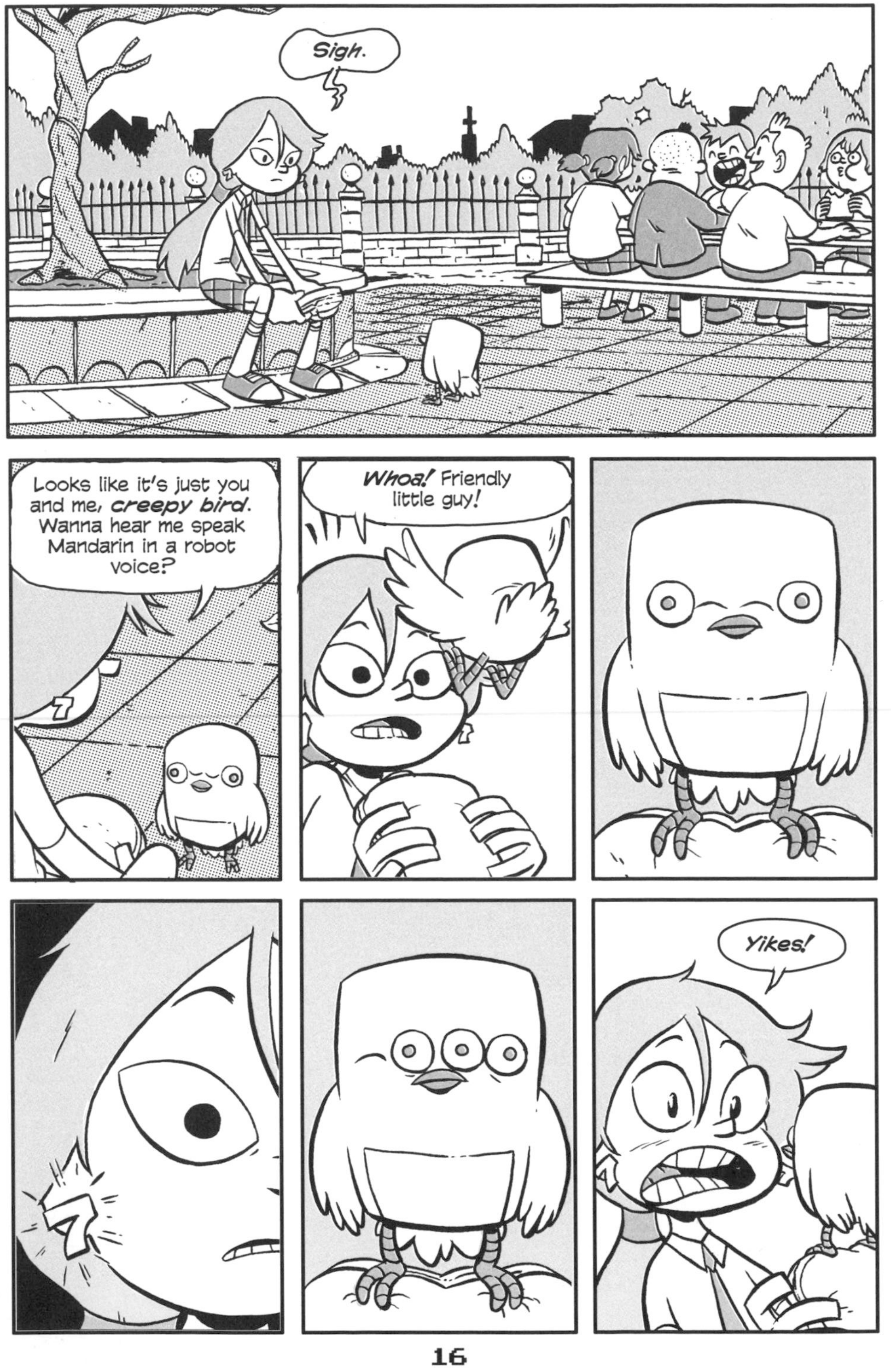
Sigh.
Looks like it's just you and me, creepy bird. Wanna hear me speak Mandarin in a robot voice?
7
Whoa! Friendly little guy!
7
Yikes!

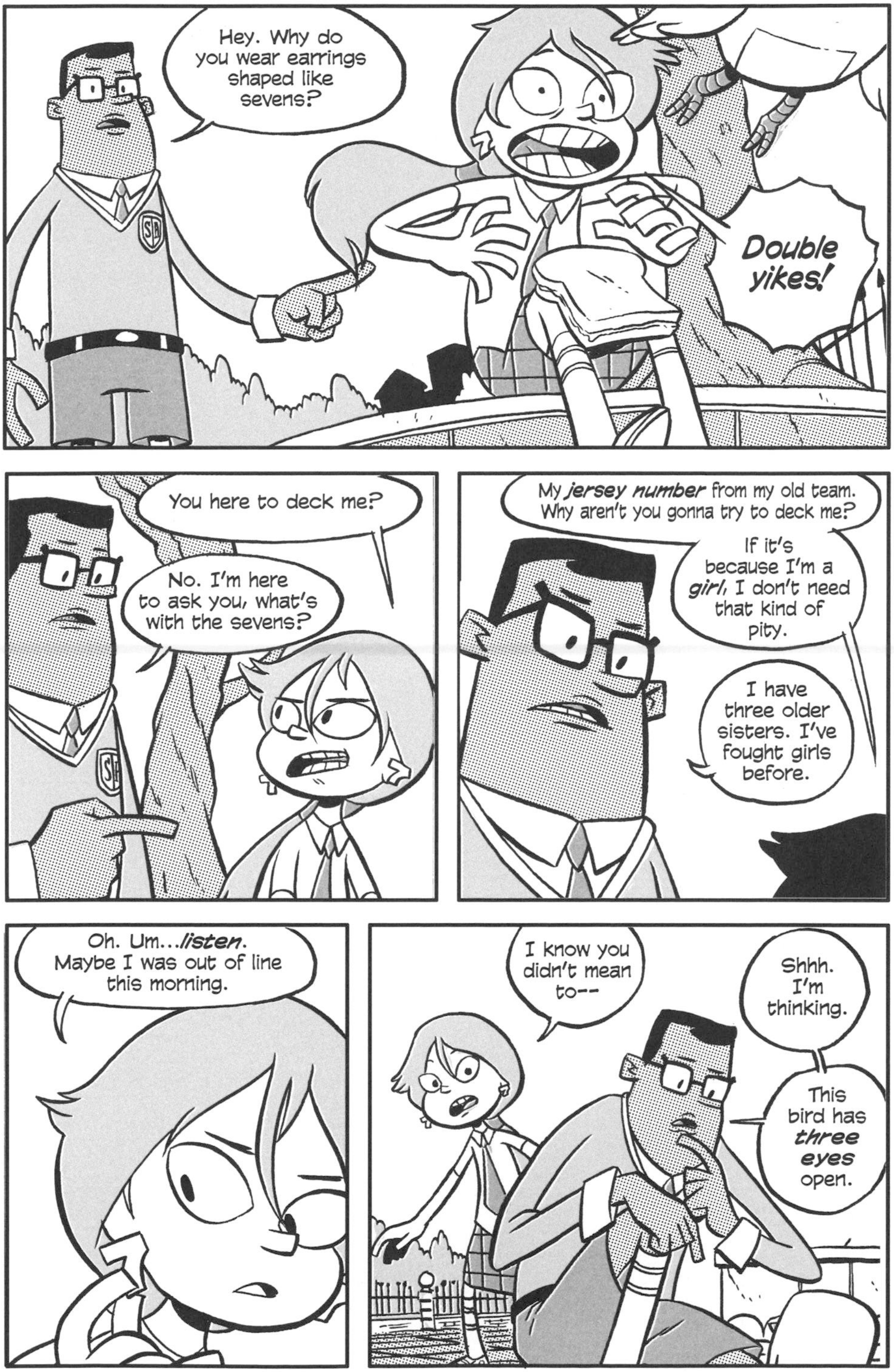

Hey. Why do you wear earrings shaped like sevens?
Double yikes!
You here to deck me?
No. I'm here to ask you, what's with the sevens?
My *jersey number* from my old team. Why aren't you gonna try to deck me?
If it's because I'm a *girl*, I don't need that kind of pity.
I have three older sisters. I've fought girls before.
Oh. Um...*listen*. Maybe I was out of line this morning.
I know you didn't mean to--
Shhh. I'm thinking.
This bird has *three eyes* open.

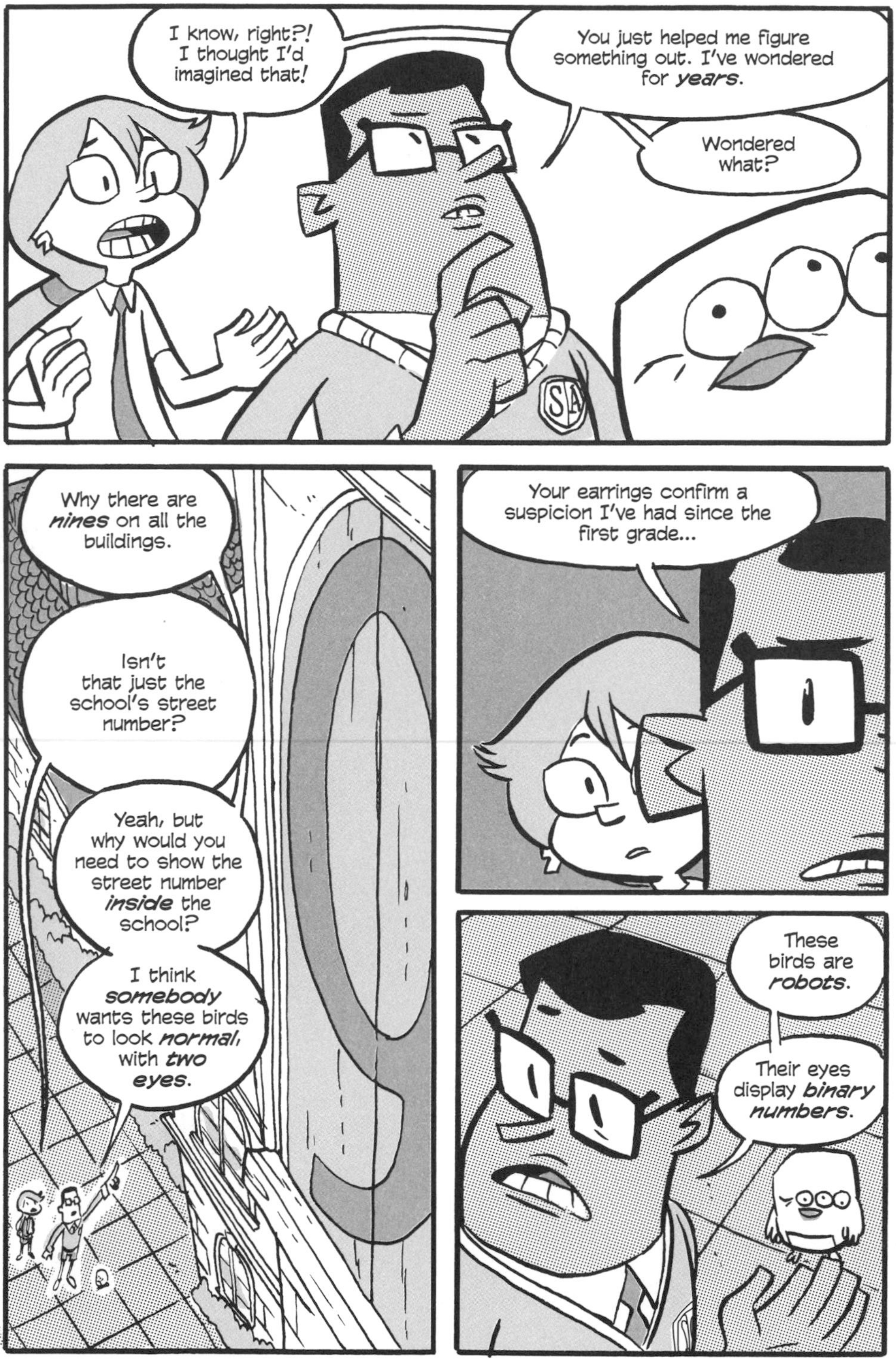
I know, right?! I thought I'd imagined that!
You just helped me figure something out. I've wondered for *years*.
Wondered what?
Why there are *nines* on all the buildings.
Isn't that just the school's street number?
Yeah, but why would you need to show the street number *inside* the school?
I think *somebody* wants these birds to look *normal*, with *two eyes*.
Your earrings confirm a suspicion I've had since the first grade...
These birds are *robots*.
Their eyes display *binary numbers*.

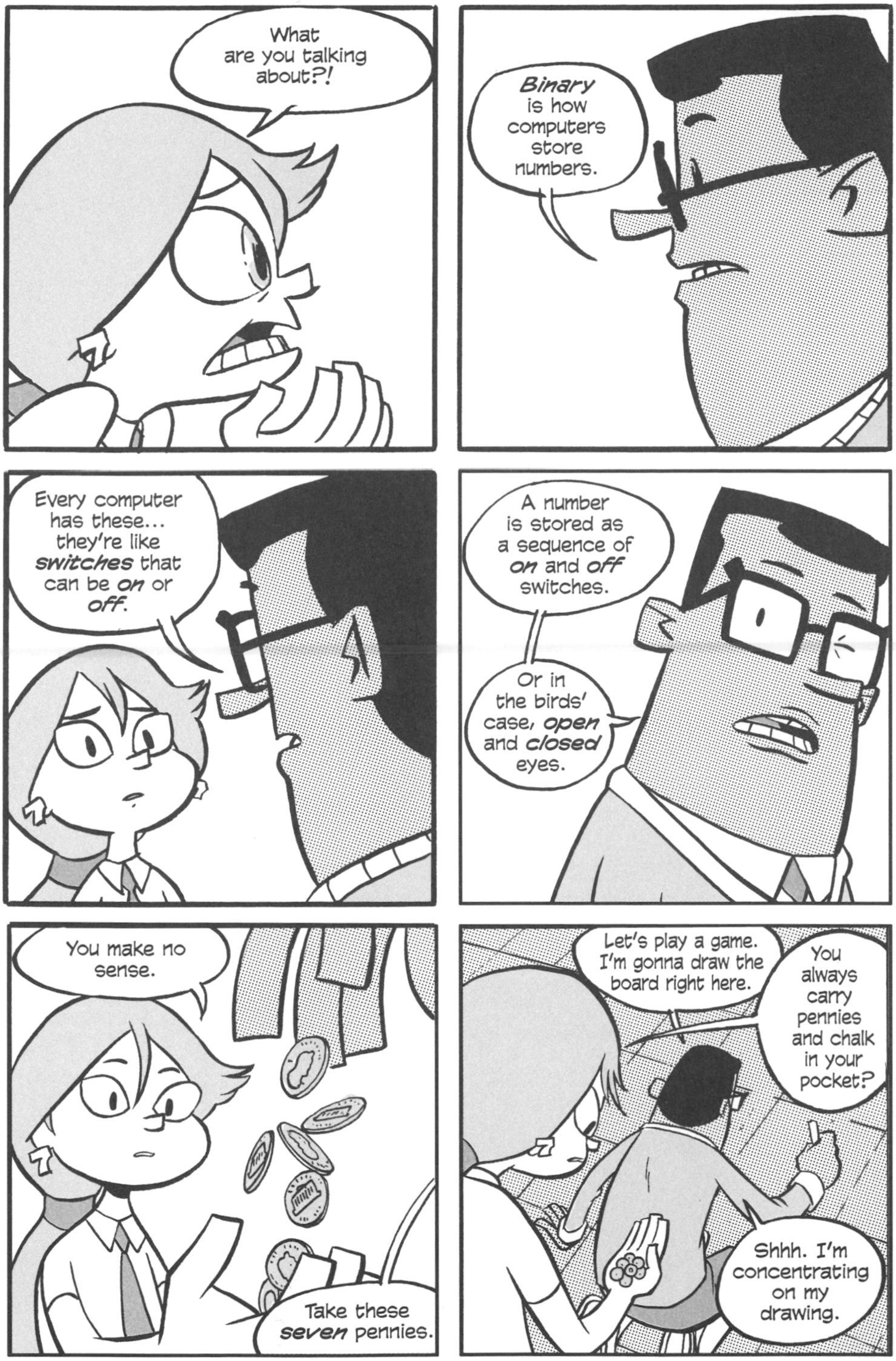
What are you talking about?!
Binary is how computers store numbers.
Every computer has these... they're like *switches* that can be *on* or *off*.
A number is stored as a sequence of *on* and *off* switches.
Or in the birds' case, *open* and *closed* eyes.
You make no sense.
Take these *seven* pennies.
Let's play a game. I'm gonna draw the board right here.
You always carry pennies and chalk in your pocket?
Shhh. I'm concentrating on my drawing.

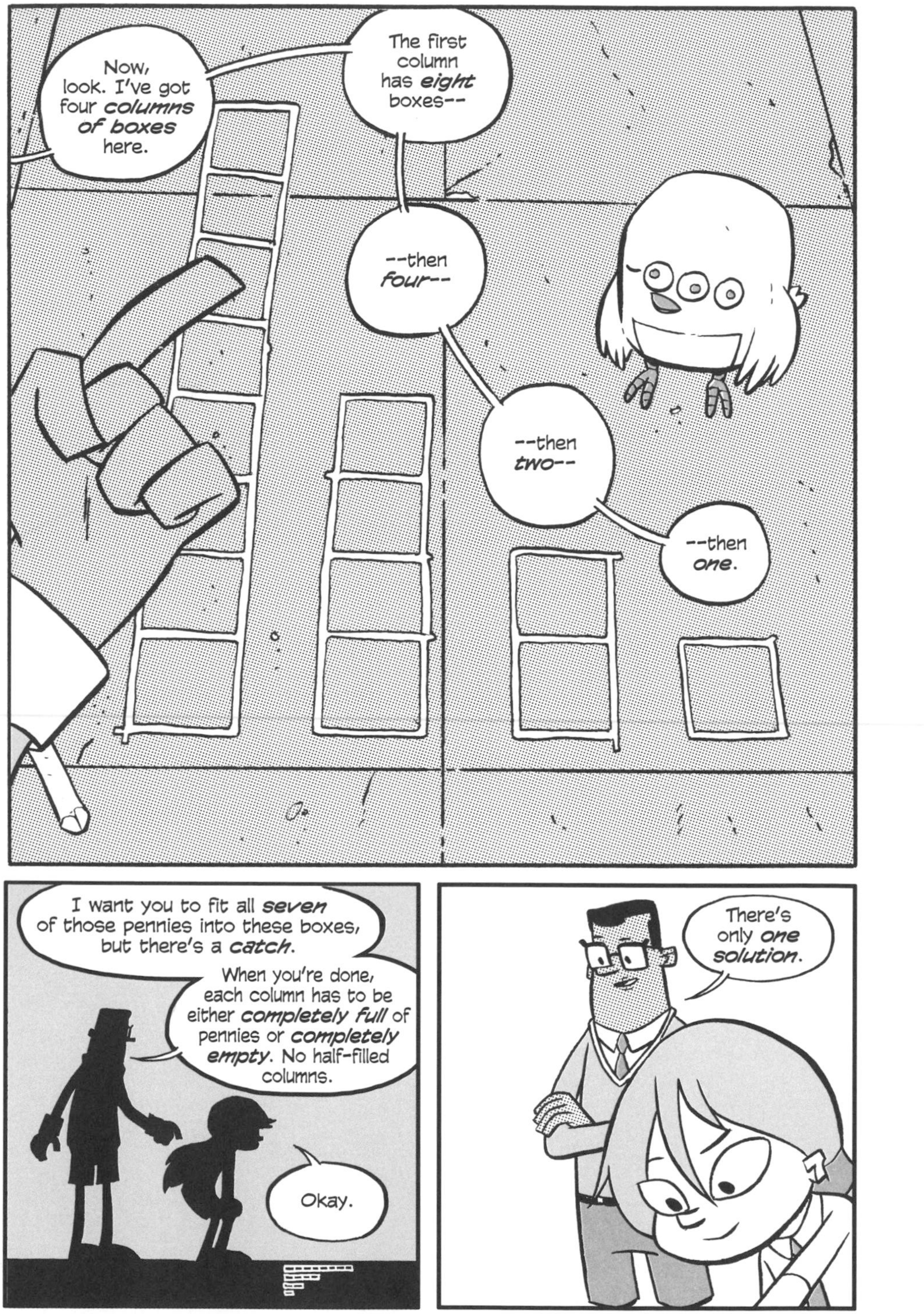
Now, look. I've got four *columns of boxes* here.
The first column has *eight* boxes--
--then *four*--
--then *two*--
--then *one*.
I want you to fit all *seven* of those pennies into these boxes, but there's a *catch*.
When you're done, each column has to be either *completely full* of pennies or *completely empty*. No half-filled columns.
Okay.
There's only *one solution*.

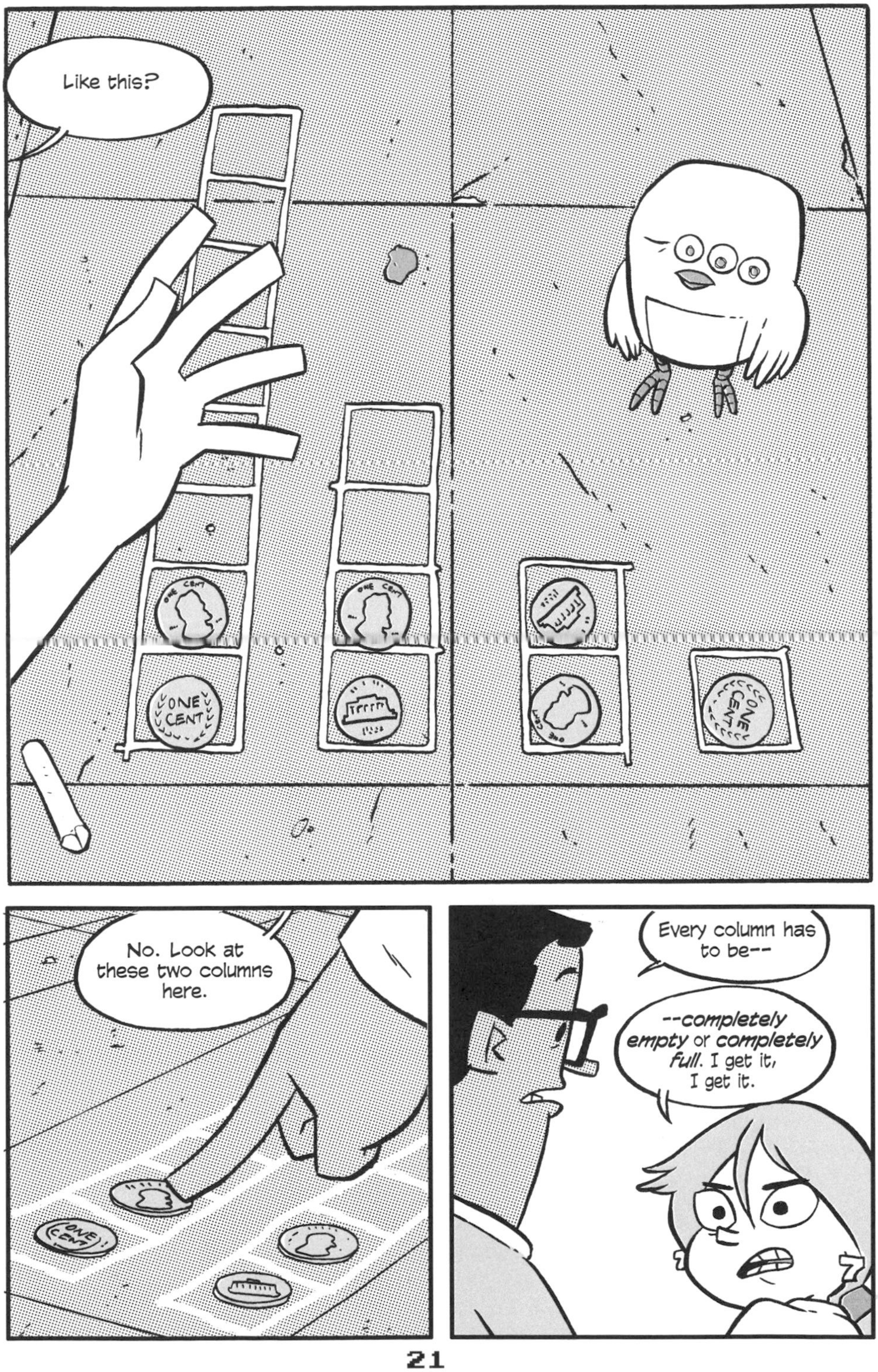
Like this?
ONE CENT
No. Look at these two columns here.
Every column has to be--
--completely empty or completely full. I get it, I get it.

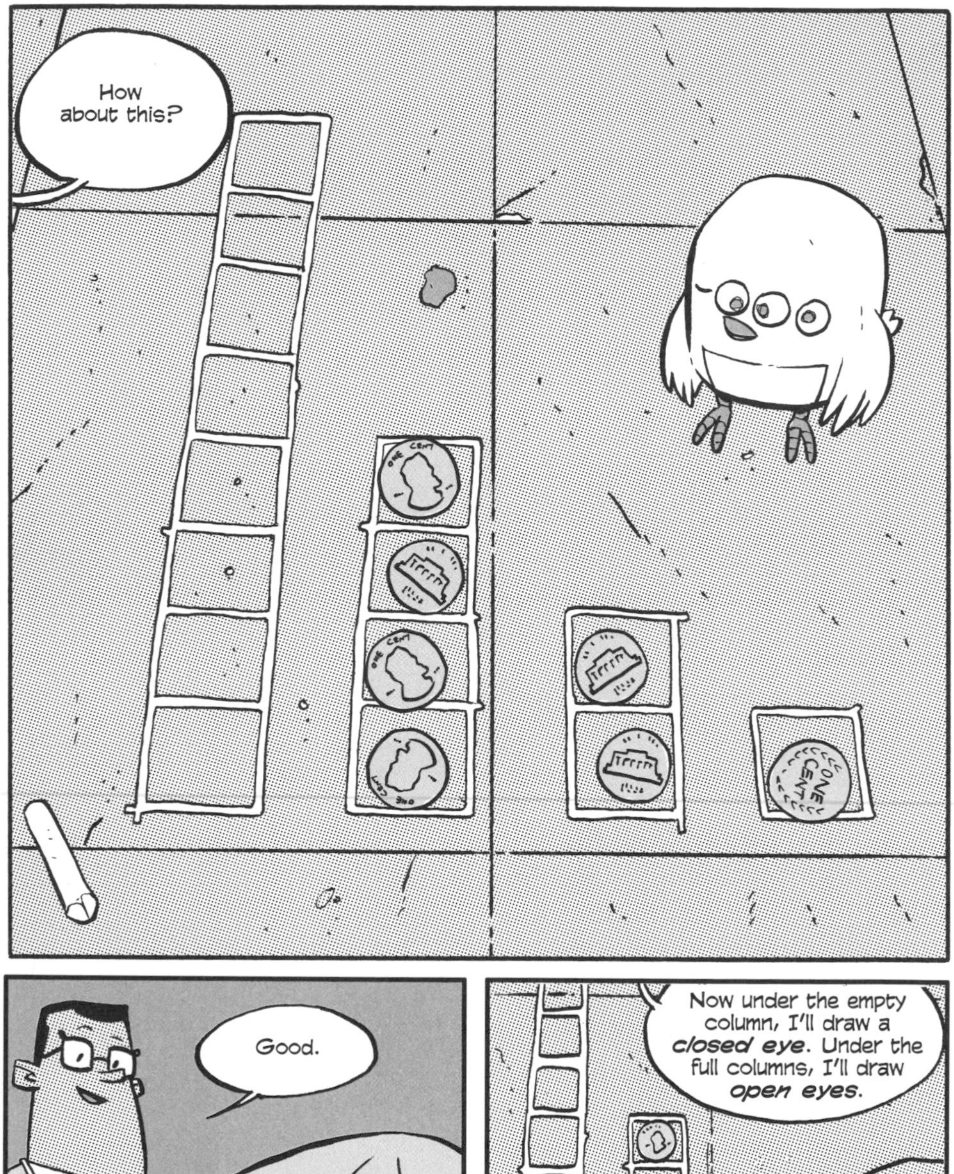
How about this?
ONE CENT
Good.
Now under the empty column, I'll draw a *closed eye*. Under the full columns, I'll draw *open eyes*.

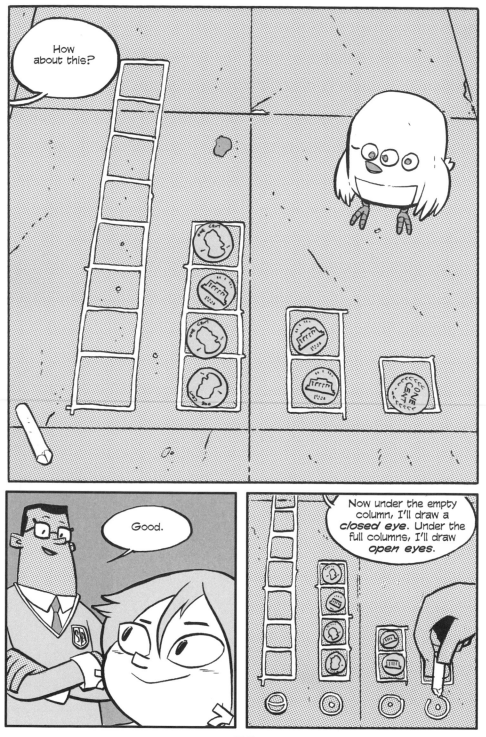

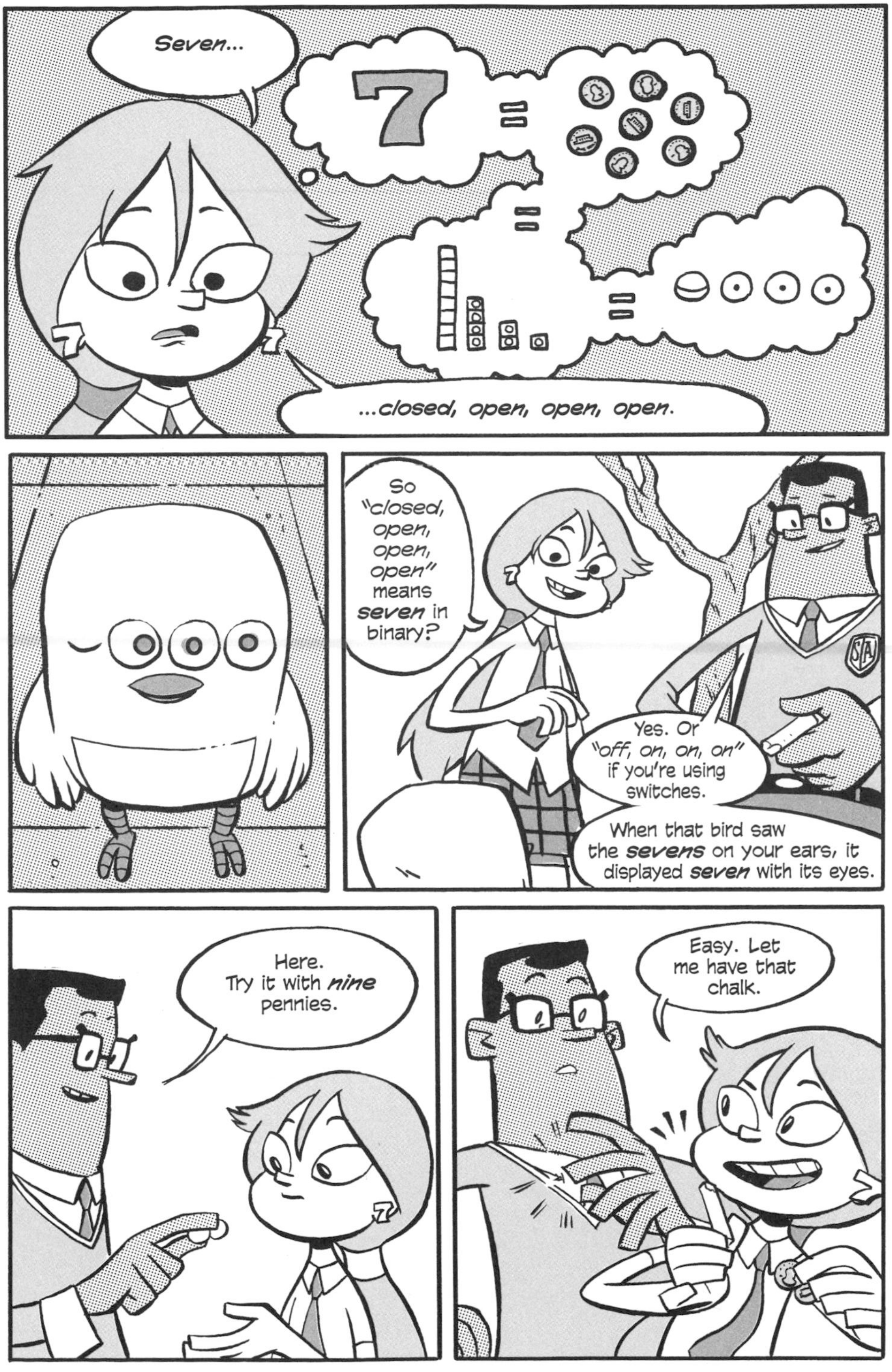

Seven...
7
...closed, open, open, open.
So "closed, open, open, open" means *seven* in binary?
Yes. Or "off, on, on, on" if you're using switches.
When that bird saw the *sevens* on your ears, it displayed *seven* with its eyes.
Here. Try it with *nine* pennies.
Easy. Let me have that chalk.

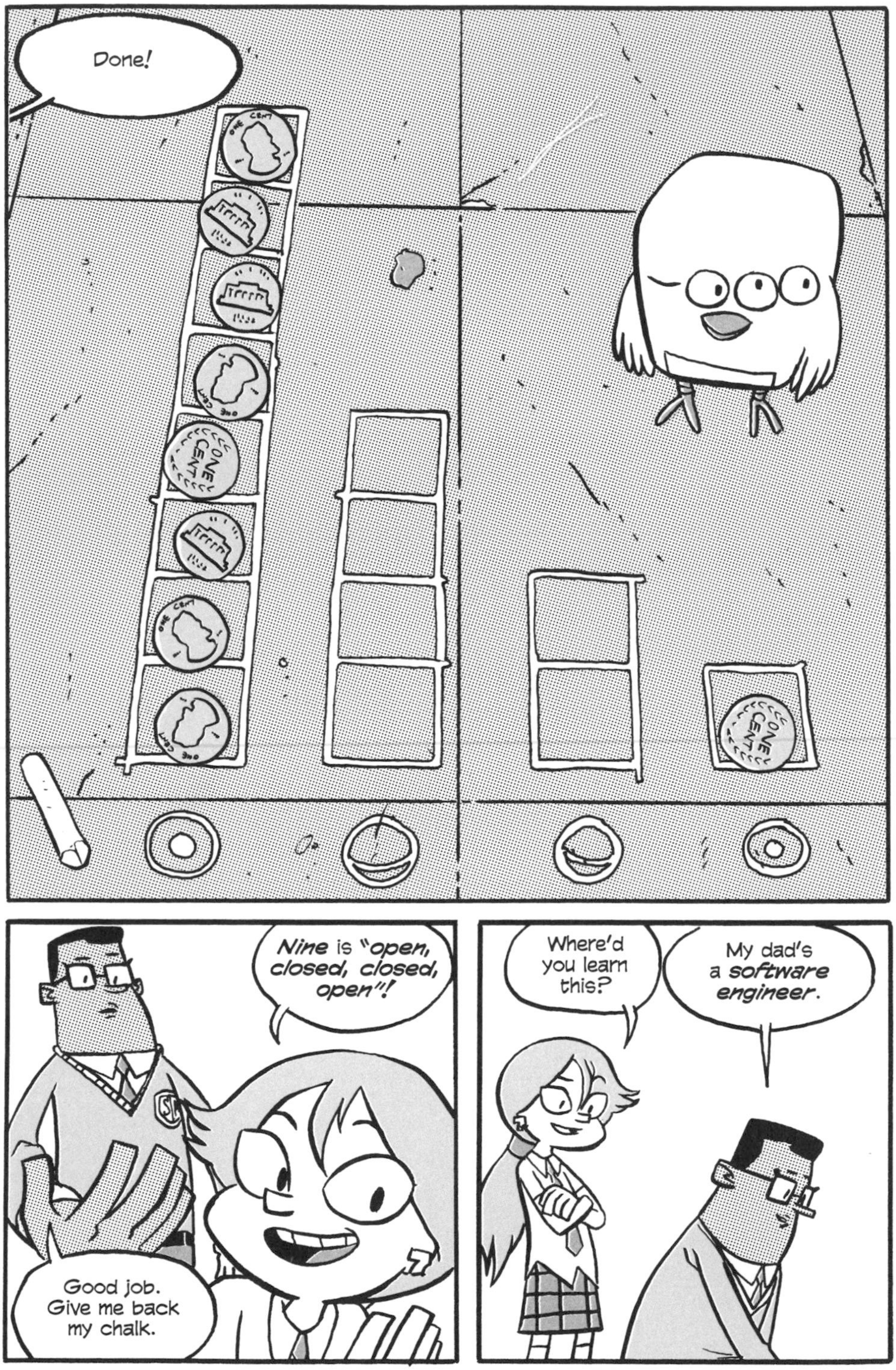

Done!
Nine is "open, closed, closed, open"!
Good job. Give me back my chalk.
Where'd you learn this?
My dad's a software engineer.

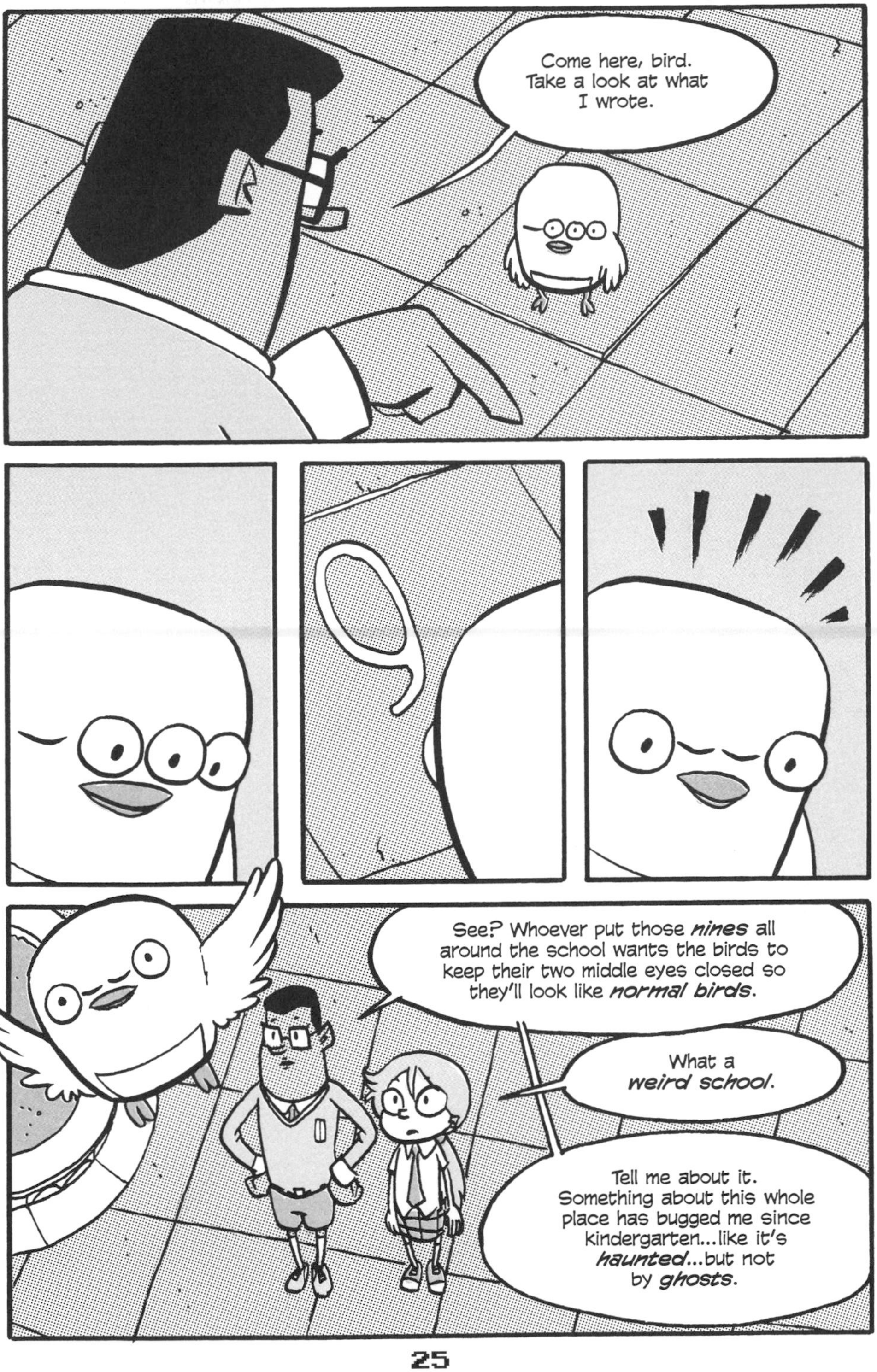
Come here, bird. Take a look at what I wrote.
See? Whoever put those *nines* all around the school wants the birds to keep their two middle eyes closed so they'll look like *normal birds*.
What a *weird school*.
Tell me about it. Something about this whole place has bugged me since kindergarten...like it's *haunted*...but not by *ghosts*.

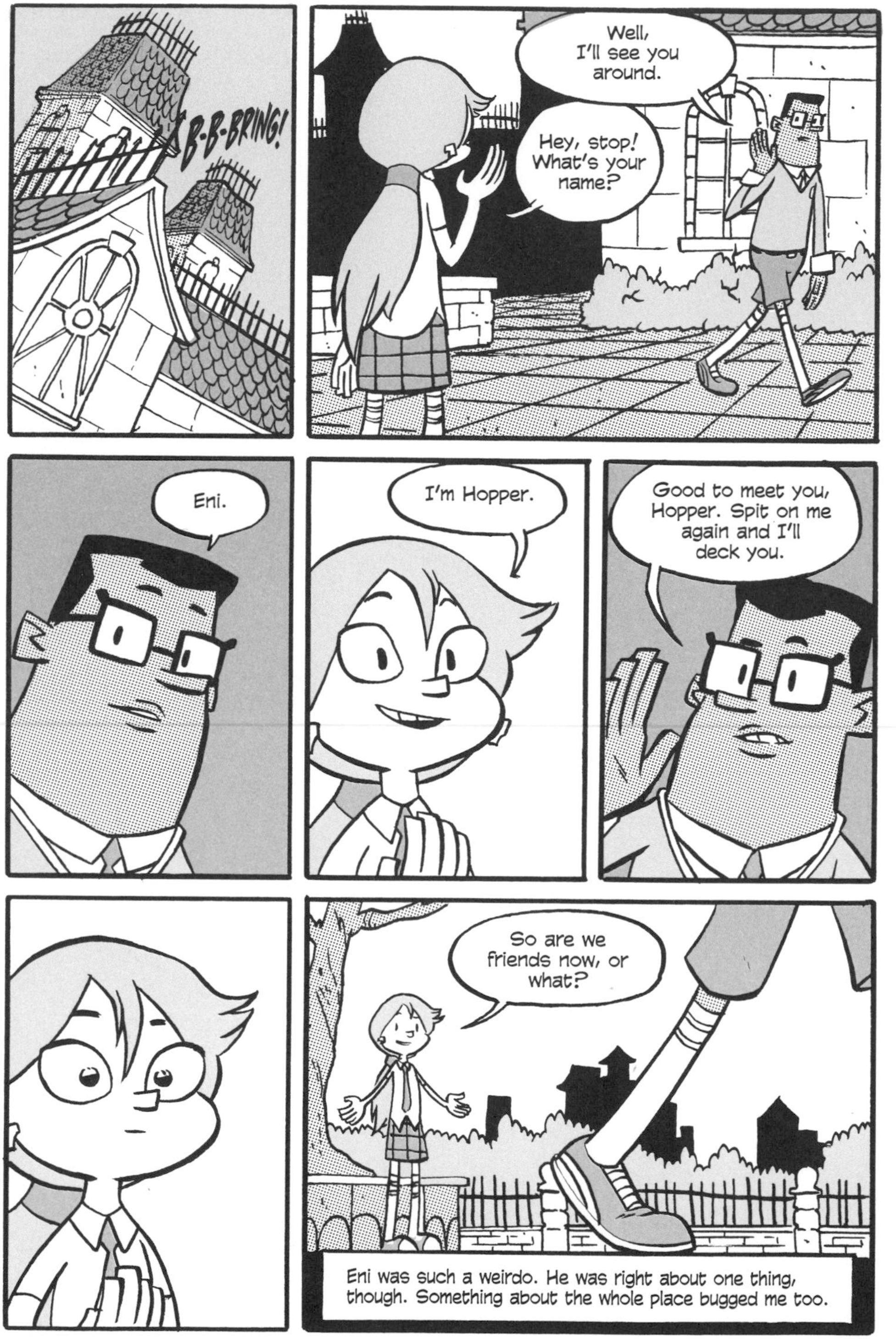
B-B-BRING!
Well, I'll see you around.
Hey, stop! What's your name?
Eni.
I'm Hopper.
Good to meet you, Hopper. Spit on me again and I'll deck you.
So are we friends now, or what?
Eni was such a weirdo. He was right about one thing, though. Something about the whole place bugged me too.

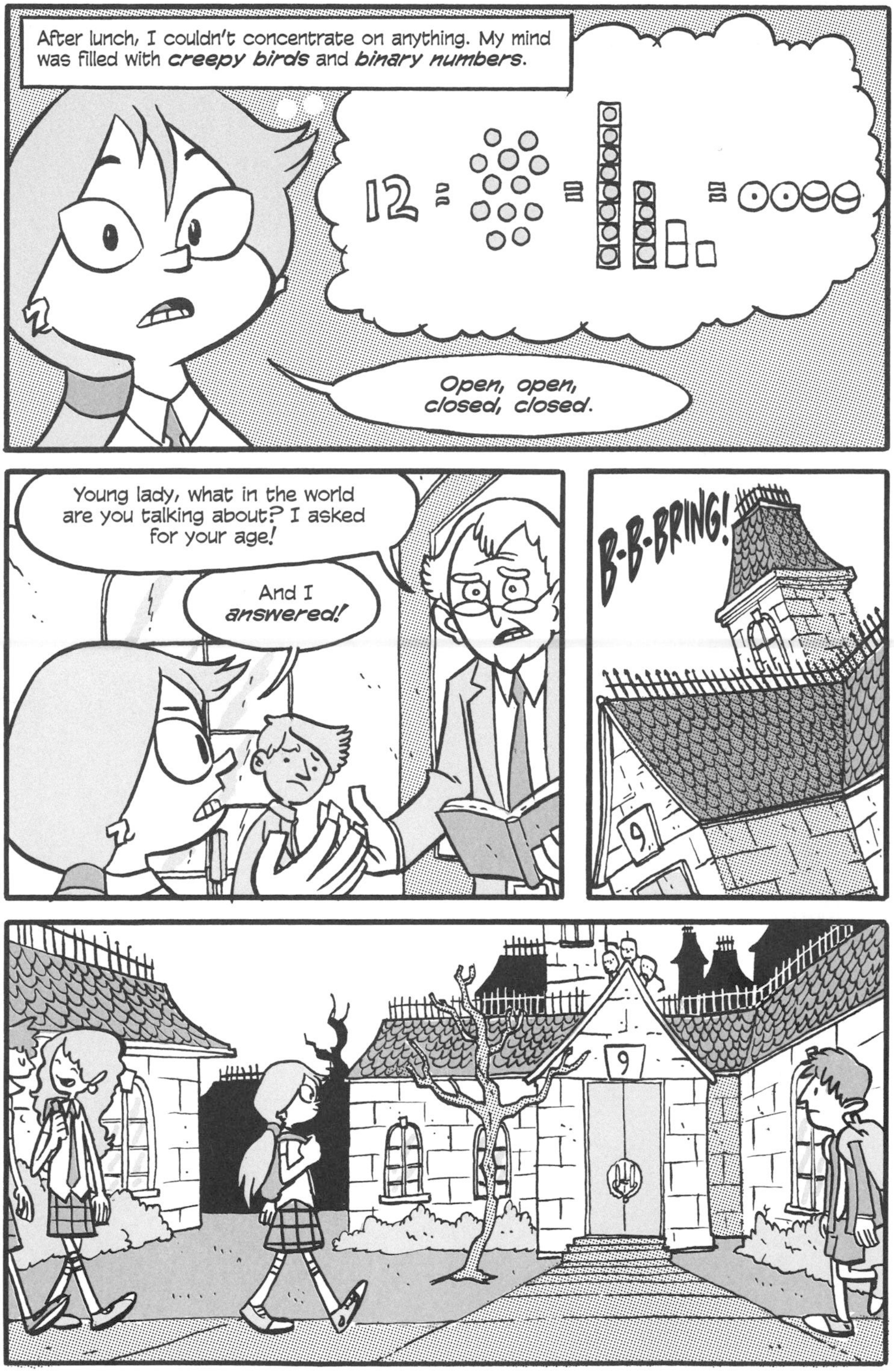
After lunch, I couldn't concentrate on anything. My mind was filled with *creepy birds* and *binary numbers*.
12 = = = 0099
Open, open, closed, closed.
Young lady, what in the world are you talking about? I asked for your age!
And I *answered!*
B-B-BRING!
9
9

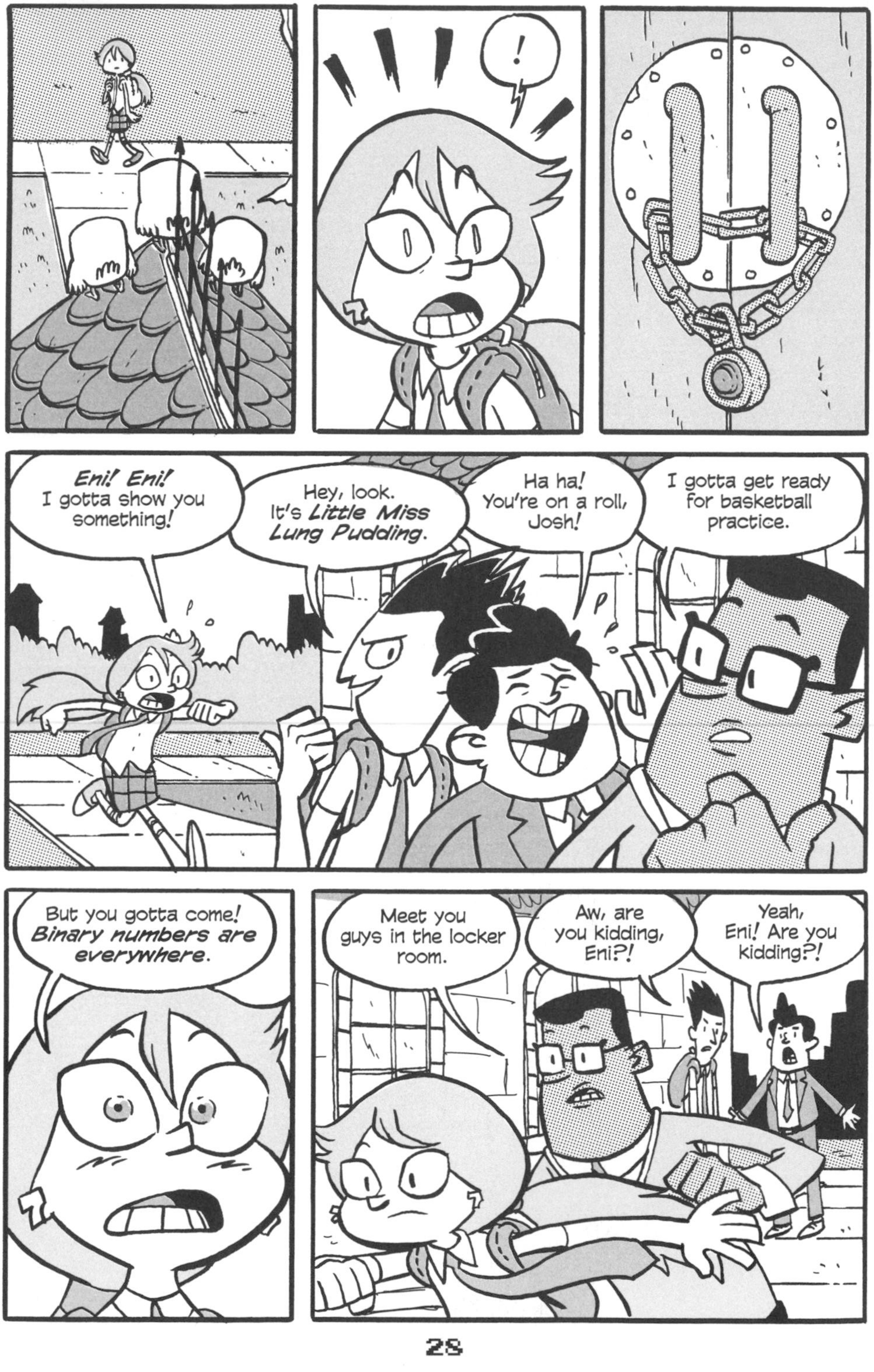
!
Eni! Eni! I gotta show you something!
Hey, look. It's Little Miss Lung Pudding.
Ha ha! You're on a roll, Josh!
I gotta get ready for basketball practice.
But you gotta come! Binary numbers are everywhere.
Meet you guys in the locker room.
Aw, are you kidding, Eni?!
Yeah, Eni! Are you kidding?!

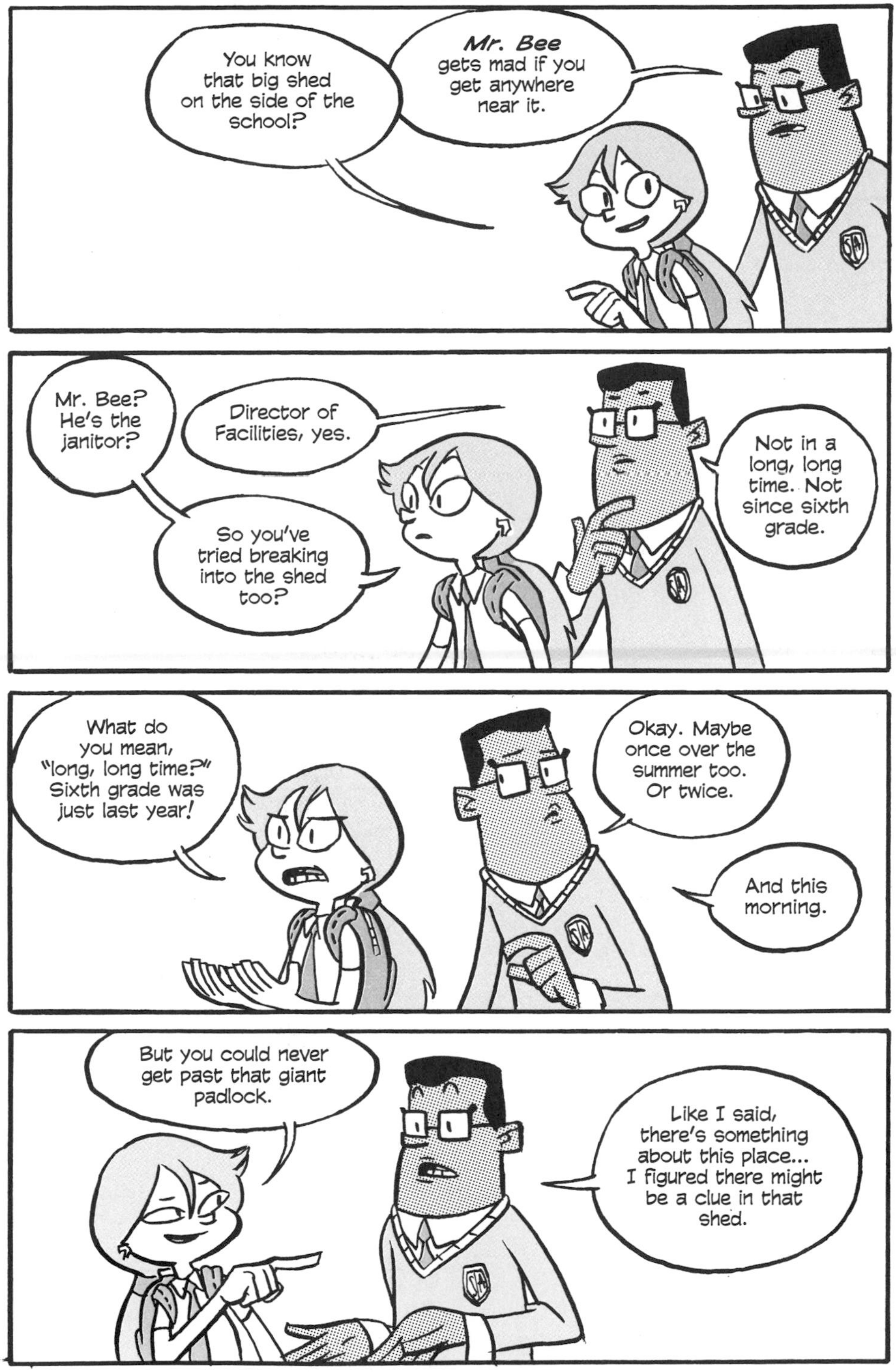
You know that big shed on the side of the school?
Mr. Bee gets mad if you get anywhere near it.
Mr. Bee? He's the janitor?
Director of Facilities, yes.
So you've tried breaking into the shed too?
Not in a long, long time. Not since sixth grade.
What do you mean, "long, long time?" Sixth grade was just last year!
Okay. Maybe once over the summer too. Or twice.
And this morning.
But you could never get past that giant padlock.
Like I said, there's something about this place... I figured there might be a clue in that shed.

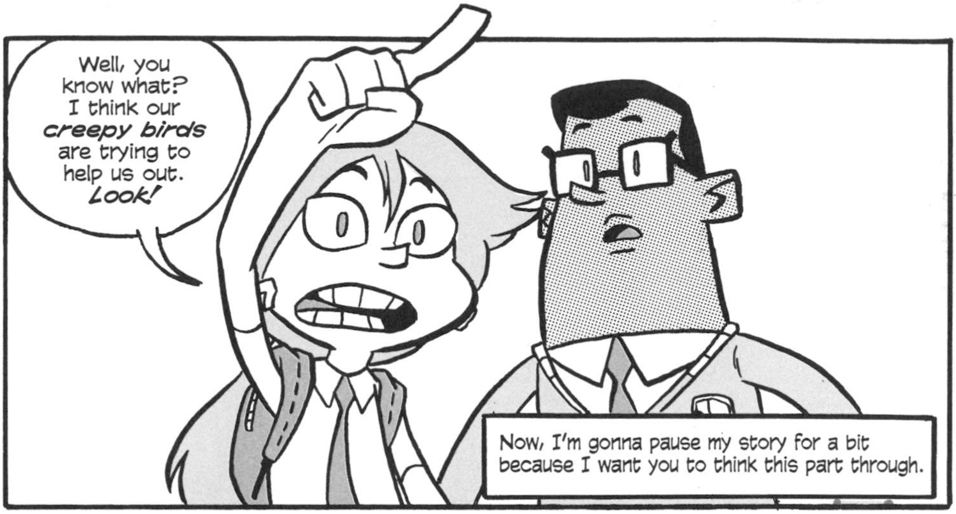
Well, you know what? I think our *creepy birds* are trying to help us out. *Look!*
Now, I'm gonna pause my story for a bit because I want you to think this part through.

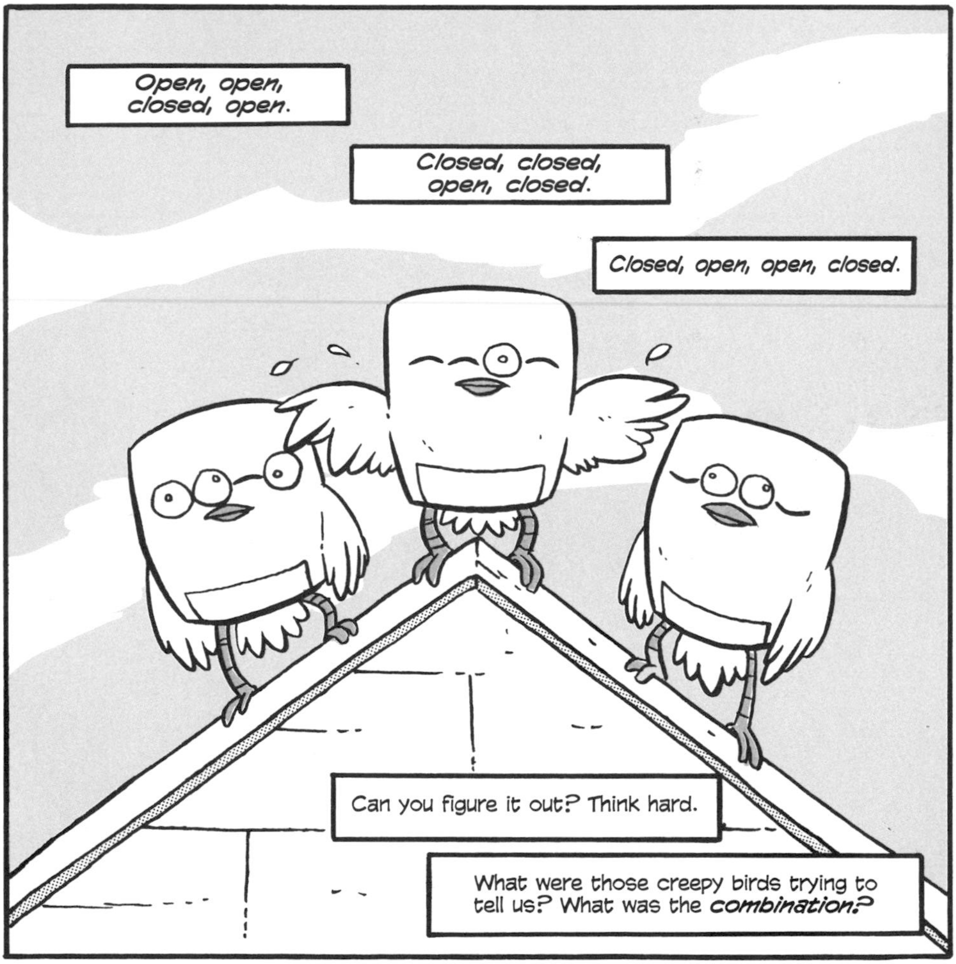
Open, open, closed, open.
Closed, closed, open, closed.
Closed, open, open, closed.
Can you figure it out? Think hard.
What were those creepy birds trying to tell us? What was the *combination?*

Chapter

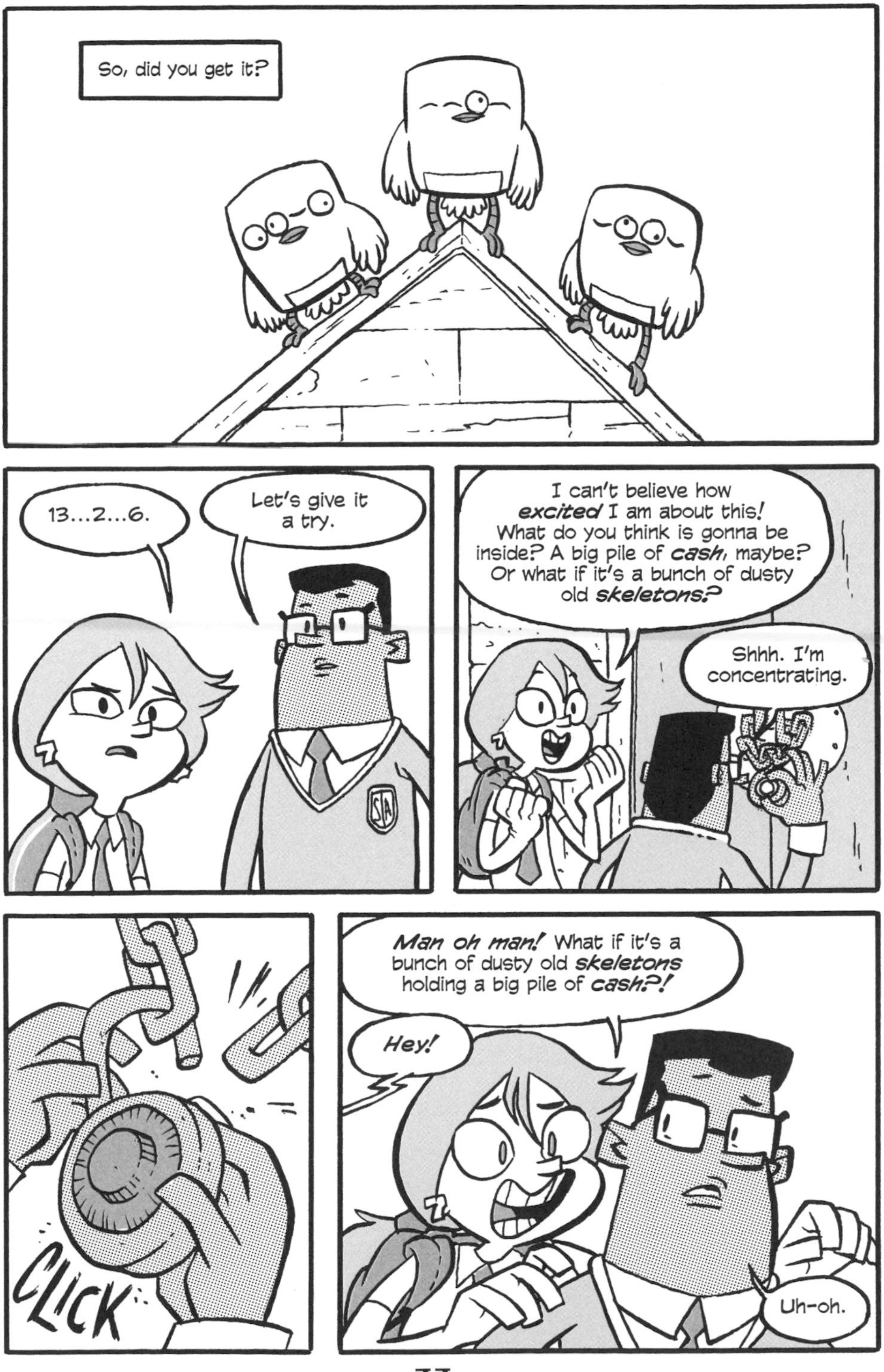
So, did you get it?
13...2...6.
Let's give it a try.
I can't believe how *excited* I am about this! What do you think is gonna be inside? A big pile of *cash*, maybe? Or what if it's a bunch of dusty old *skeletons?*
Shhh. I'm concentrating.
CLICK
Man oh man! What if it's a bunch of dusty old *skeletons* holding a big pile of *cash?!*
Hey!
Uh-oh.

35

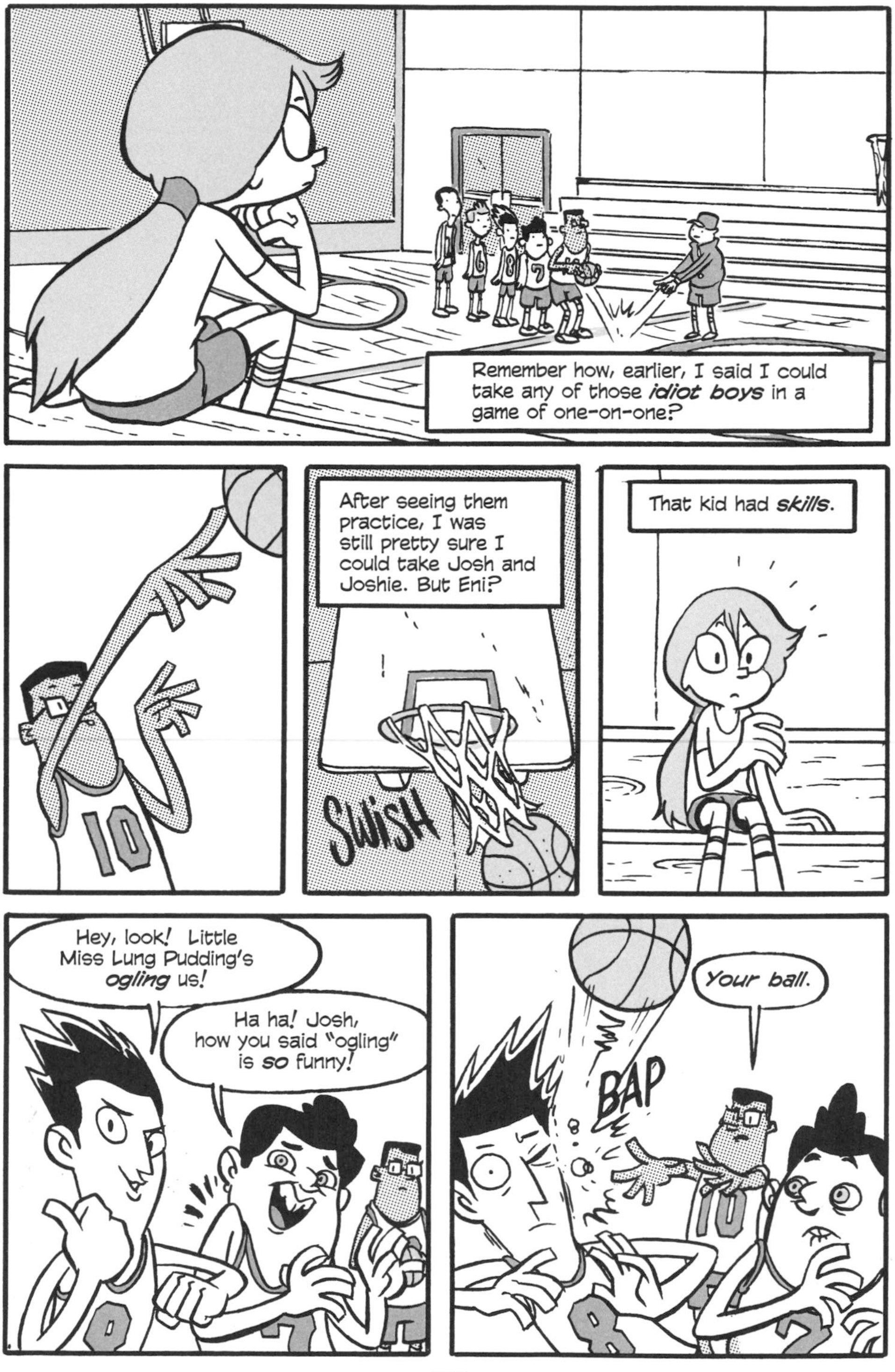
Remember how, earlier, I said I could take any of those *idiot boys* in a game of one-on-one?
After seeing them practice, I was still pretty sure I could take Josh and Joshie. But Eni?
SWISH
That kid had *skills.*
Hey, look! Little Miss Lung Pudding's *ogling* us!
Ha ha! Josh, how you said "ogling" is *so* funny!
Your ball.
BAP

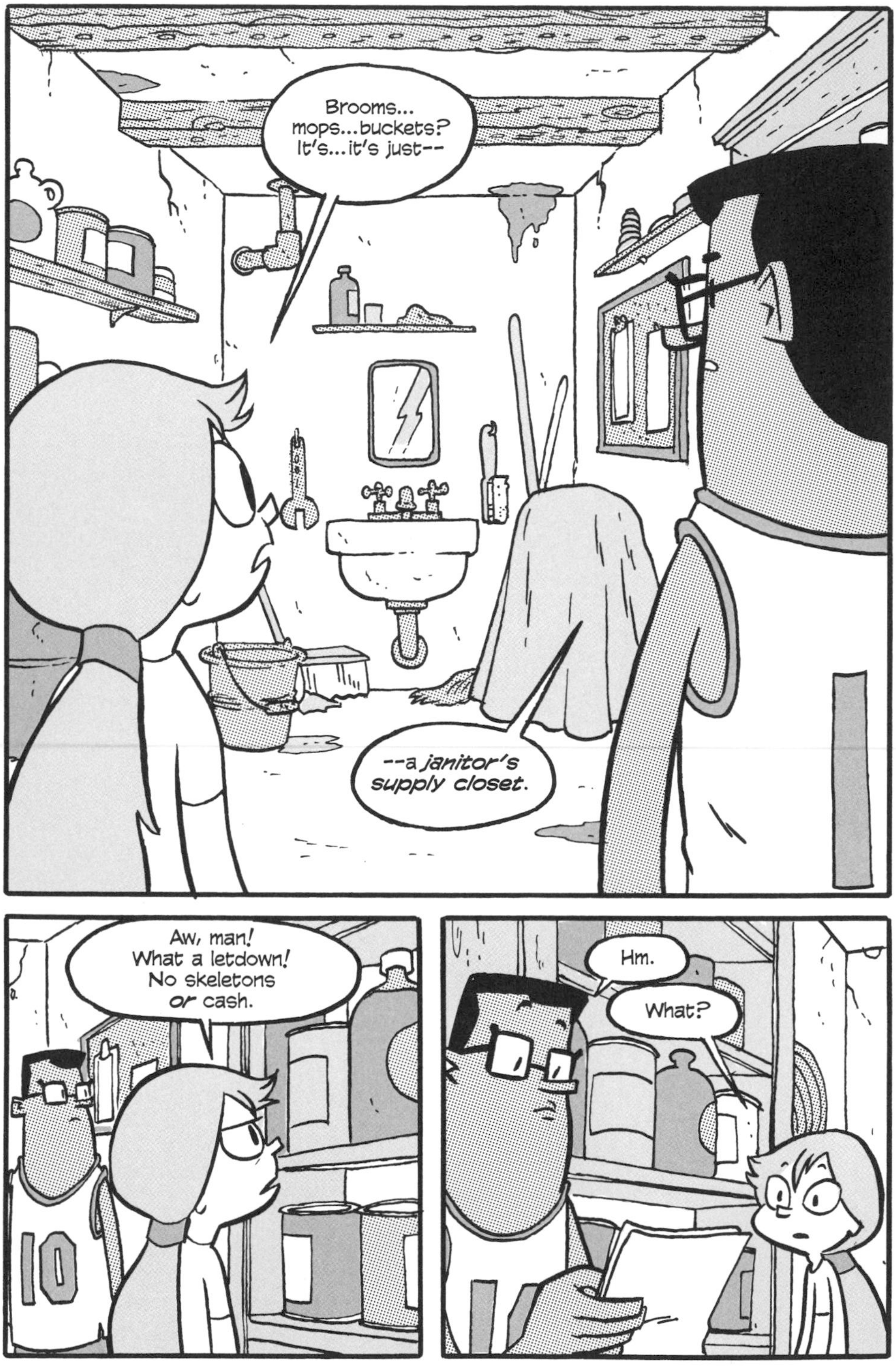
Brooms... mops...buckets? It's...it's just--
--a *janitor's supply closet*.
Aw, man! What a letdown! No skeletons *or* cash.
Hm.
What?

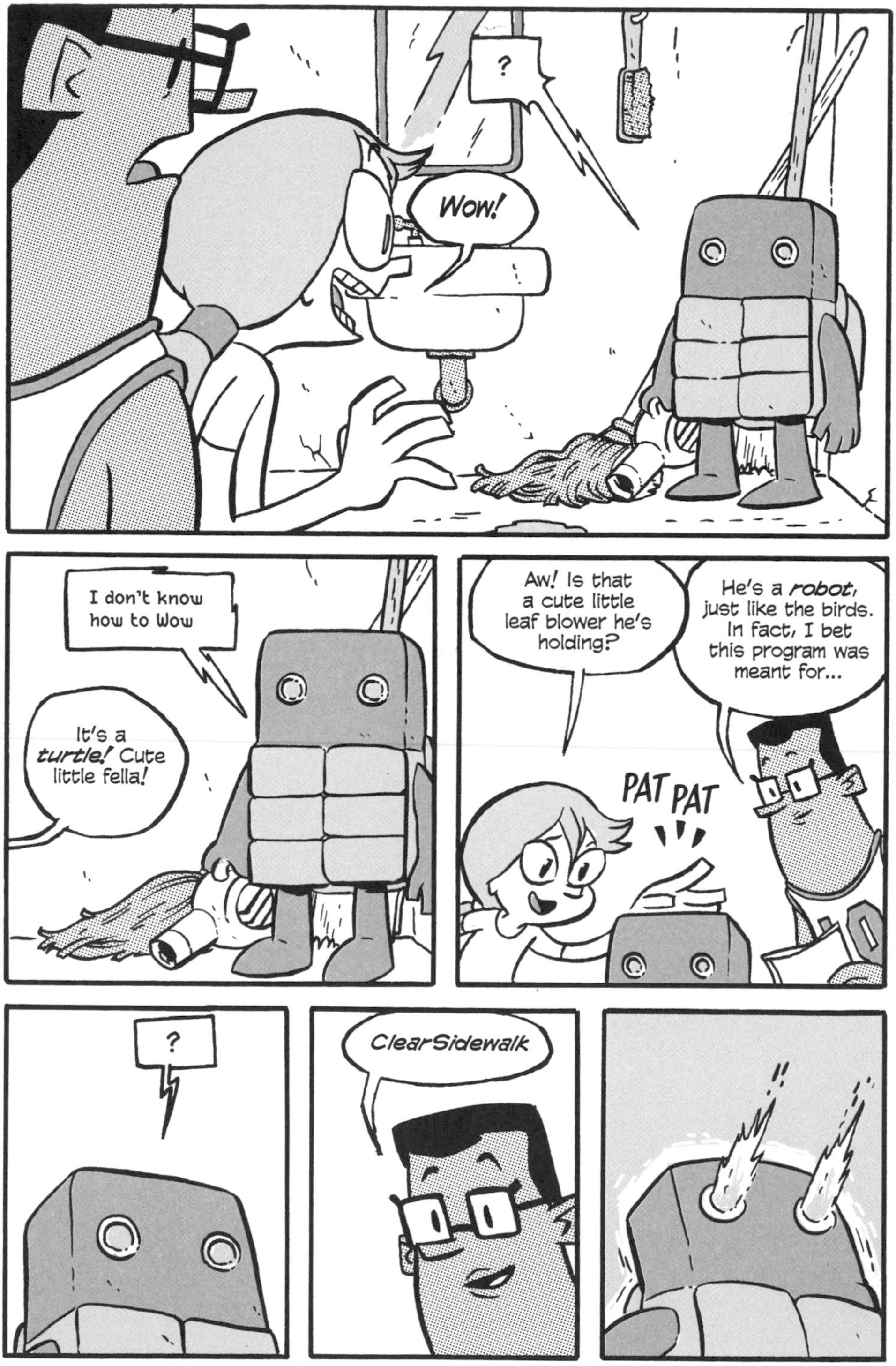
?
Wow!
I don't know how to Wow
It's a *turtle!* Cute little fella!
Aw! Is that a cute little leaf blower he's holding?
He's a *robot,* just like the birds. In fact, I bet this program was meant for...
PAT PAT
?
ClearSidewalk

41

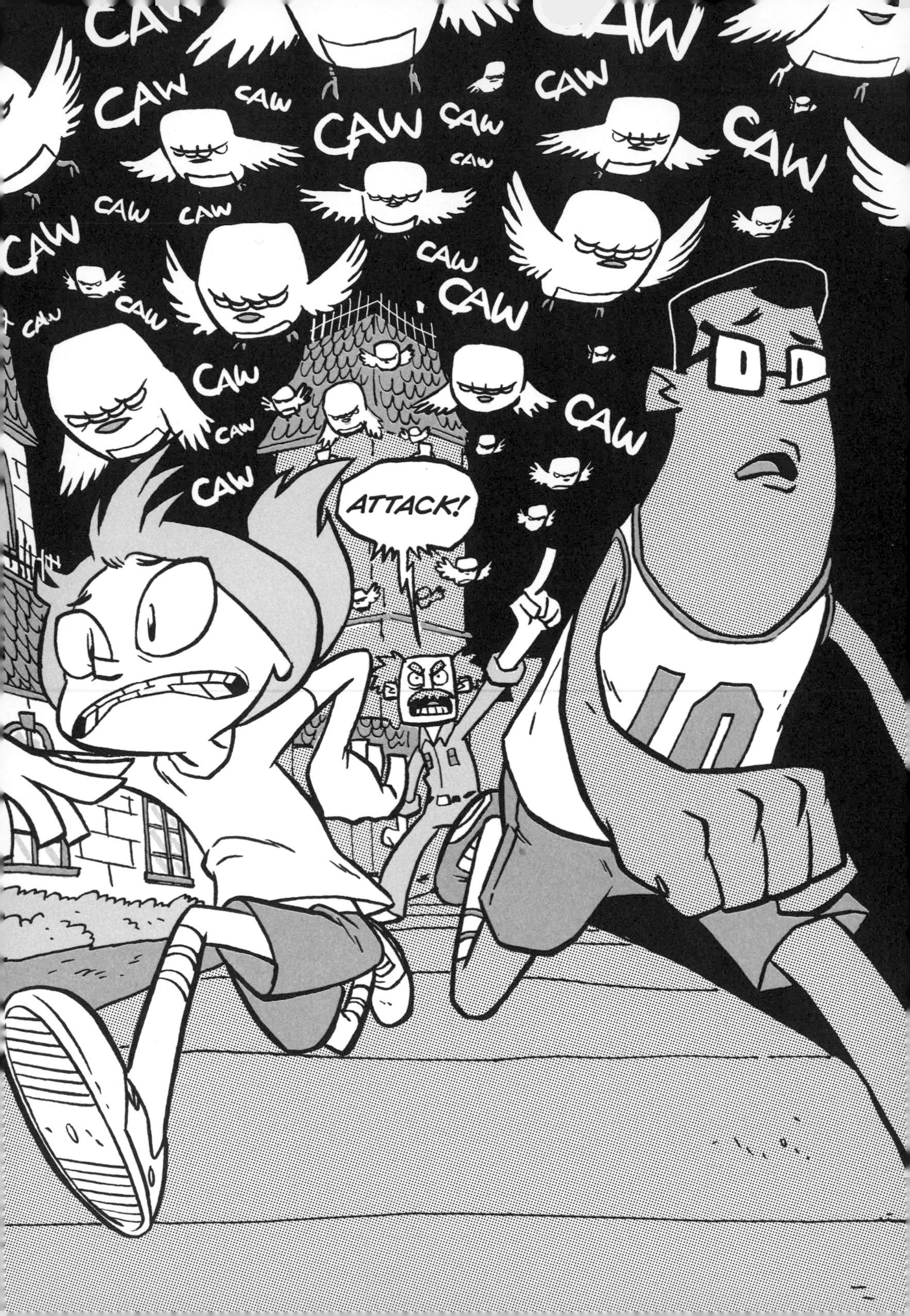
CAW
CAW
CAW
CAW
CAW
CAW
CAW
CAW
CAW
CAW
CAW
CAW
CAW
CAW
CAW
CAW
CAW
CAW
ATTACK!

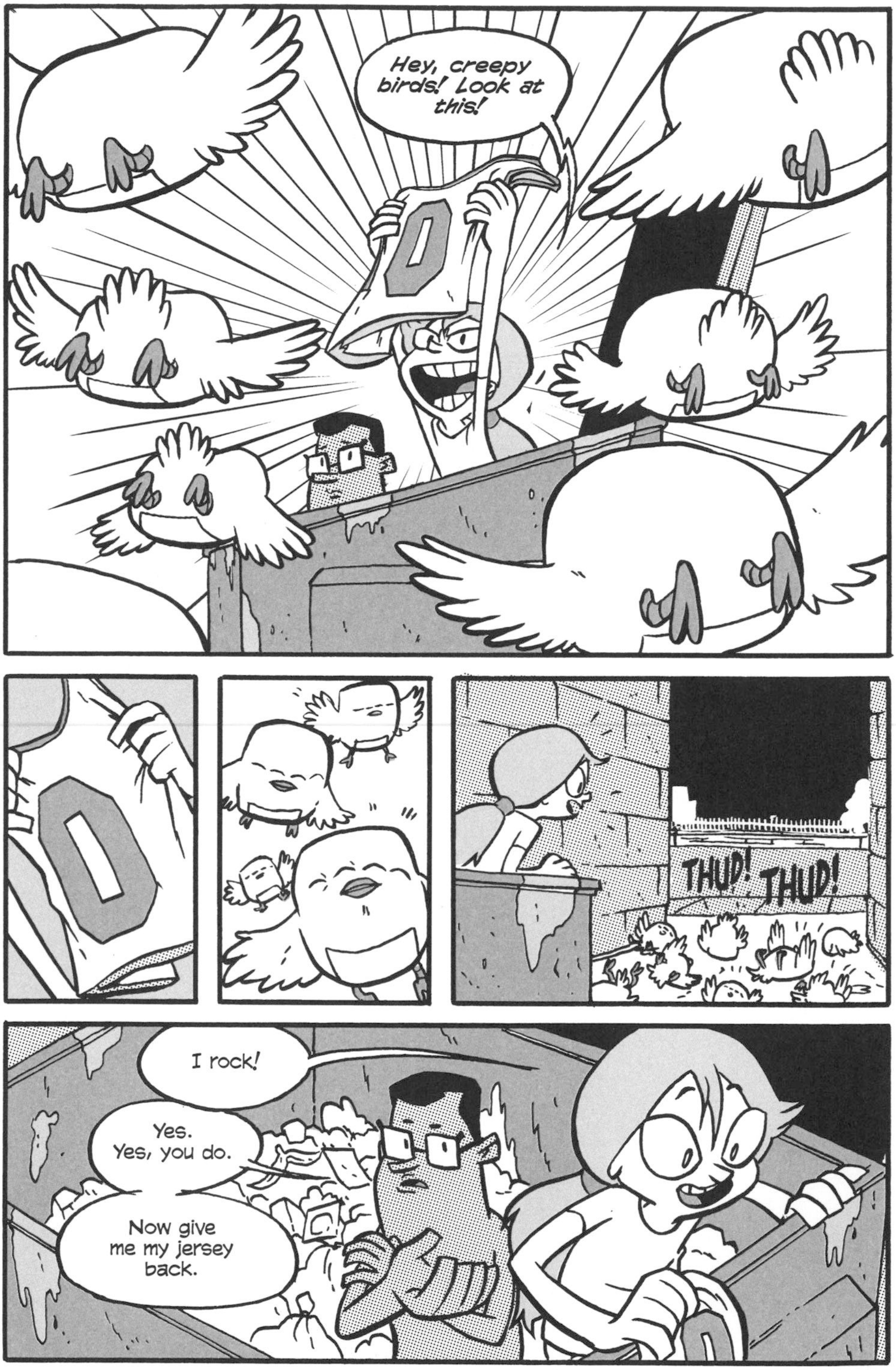
Hey, creepy birds! Look at this!
THUD! THUD!
I rock!
Yes. Yes, you do.
Now give me my jersey back.

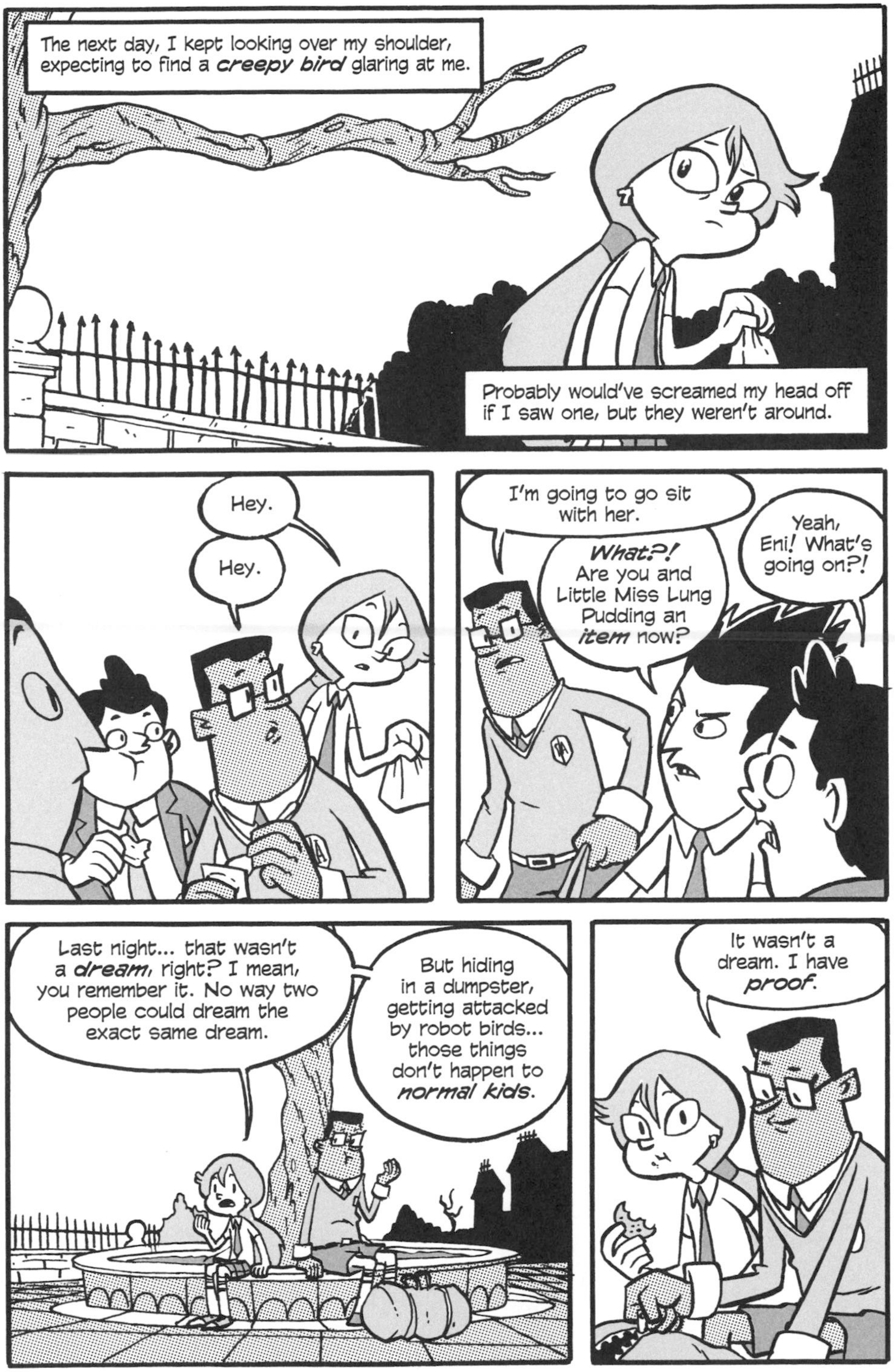
The next day, I kept looking over my shoulder, expecting to find a *creepy bird* glaring at me.
Probably would've screamed my head off if I saw one, but they weren't around.
Hey.
Hey.
I'm going to go sit with her.
What?! Are you and Little Miss Lung Pudding an *item* now?
Yeah, Eni! What's going on?!
Last night... that wasn't a *dream*, right? I mean, you remember it. No way two people could dream the exact same dream.
But hiding in a dumpster, getting attacked by robot birds... those things don't happen to *normal kids*.
It wasn't a dream. I have *proof*.

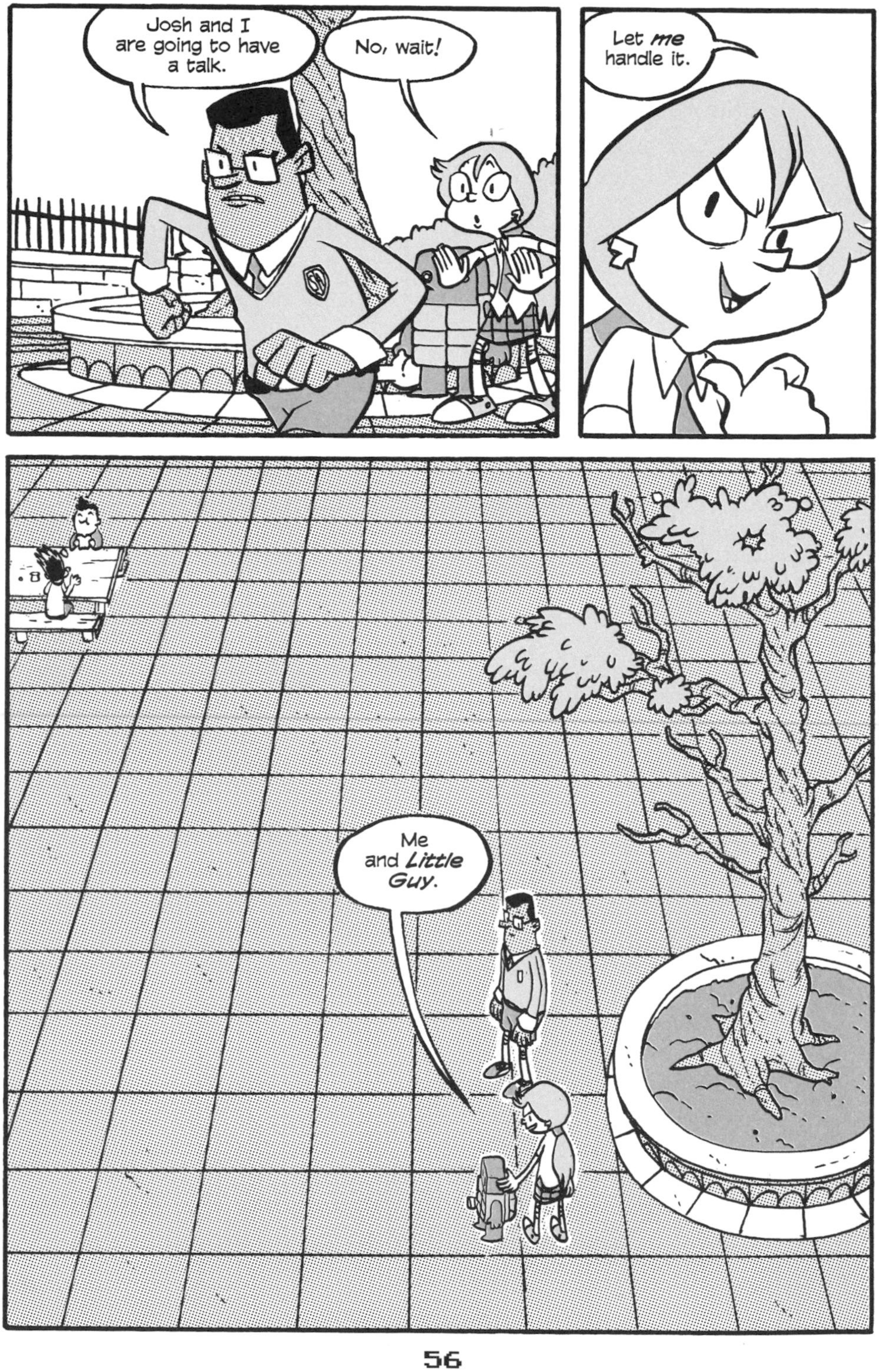

Josh and I are going to have a talk.
No, wait!
Let *me* handle it.
Me and *Little Guy*.

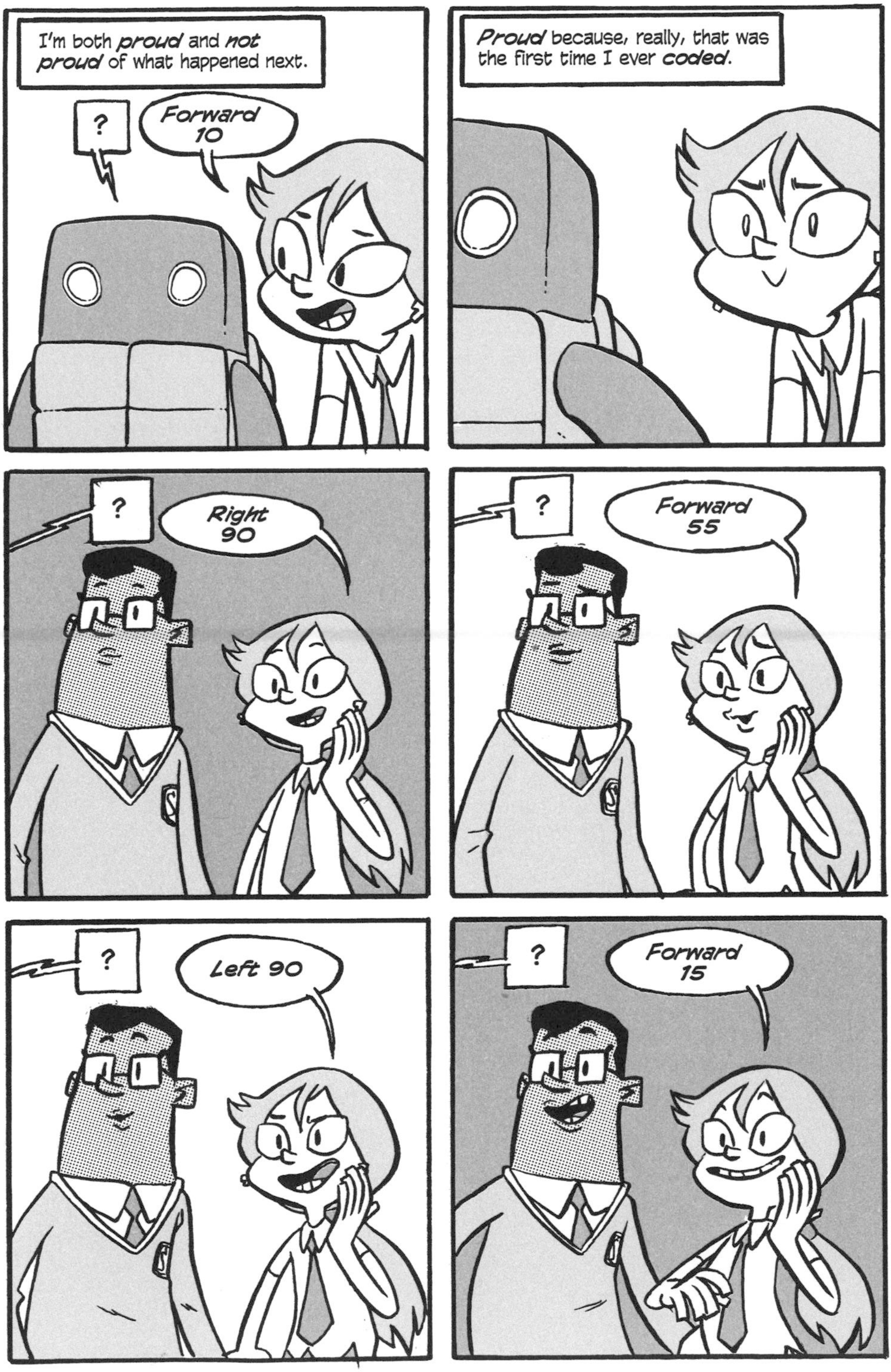
I'm both *proud* and *not proud* of what happened next.
?
Forward 10
Proud because, really, that was the first time I ever *coded*.
?
Right 90
?
Forward 55
?
Left 90
?
Forward 15

58

Chapter

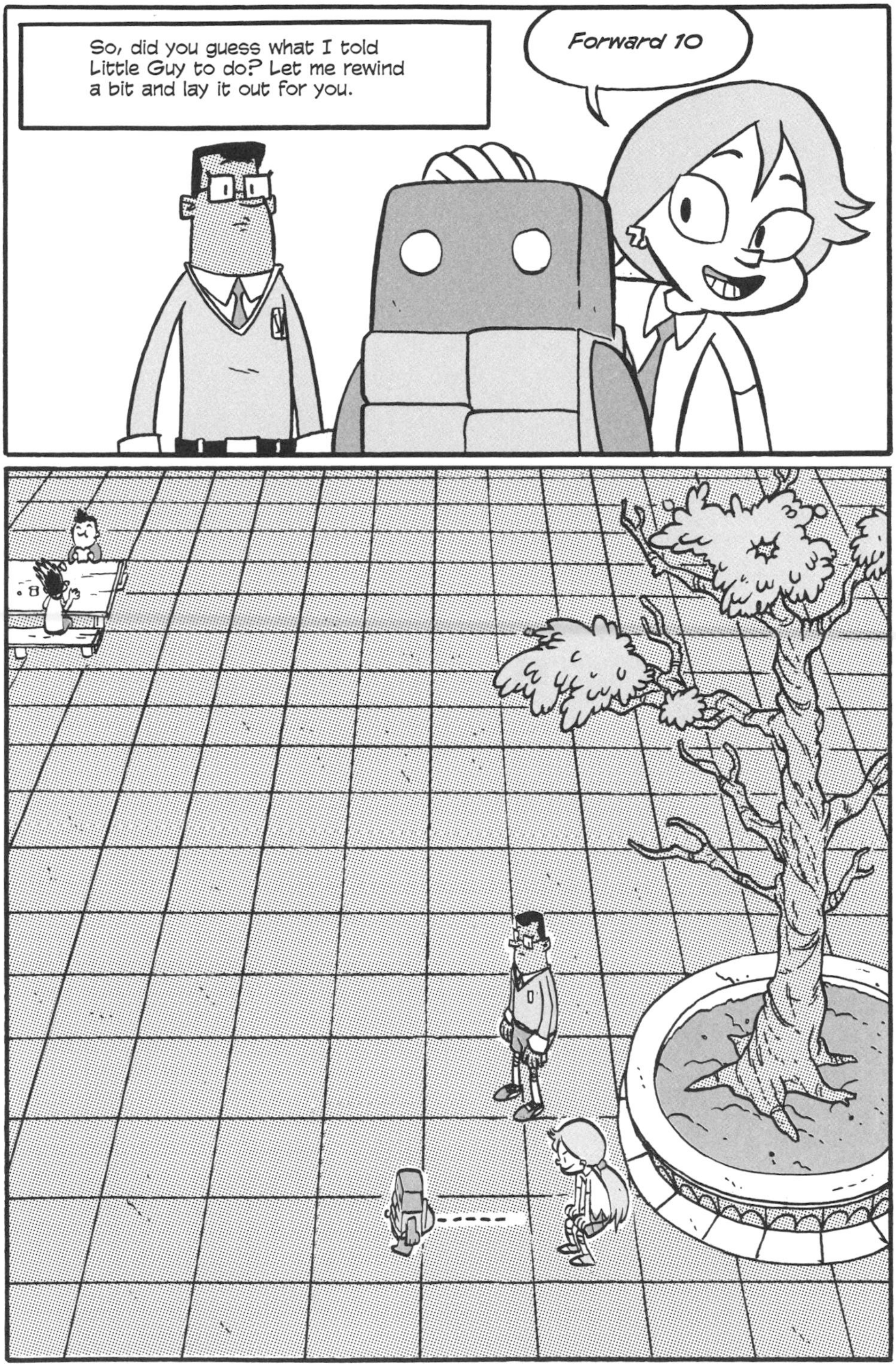
So, did you guess what I told Little Guy to do? Let me rewind a bit and lay it out for you.
Forward 10

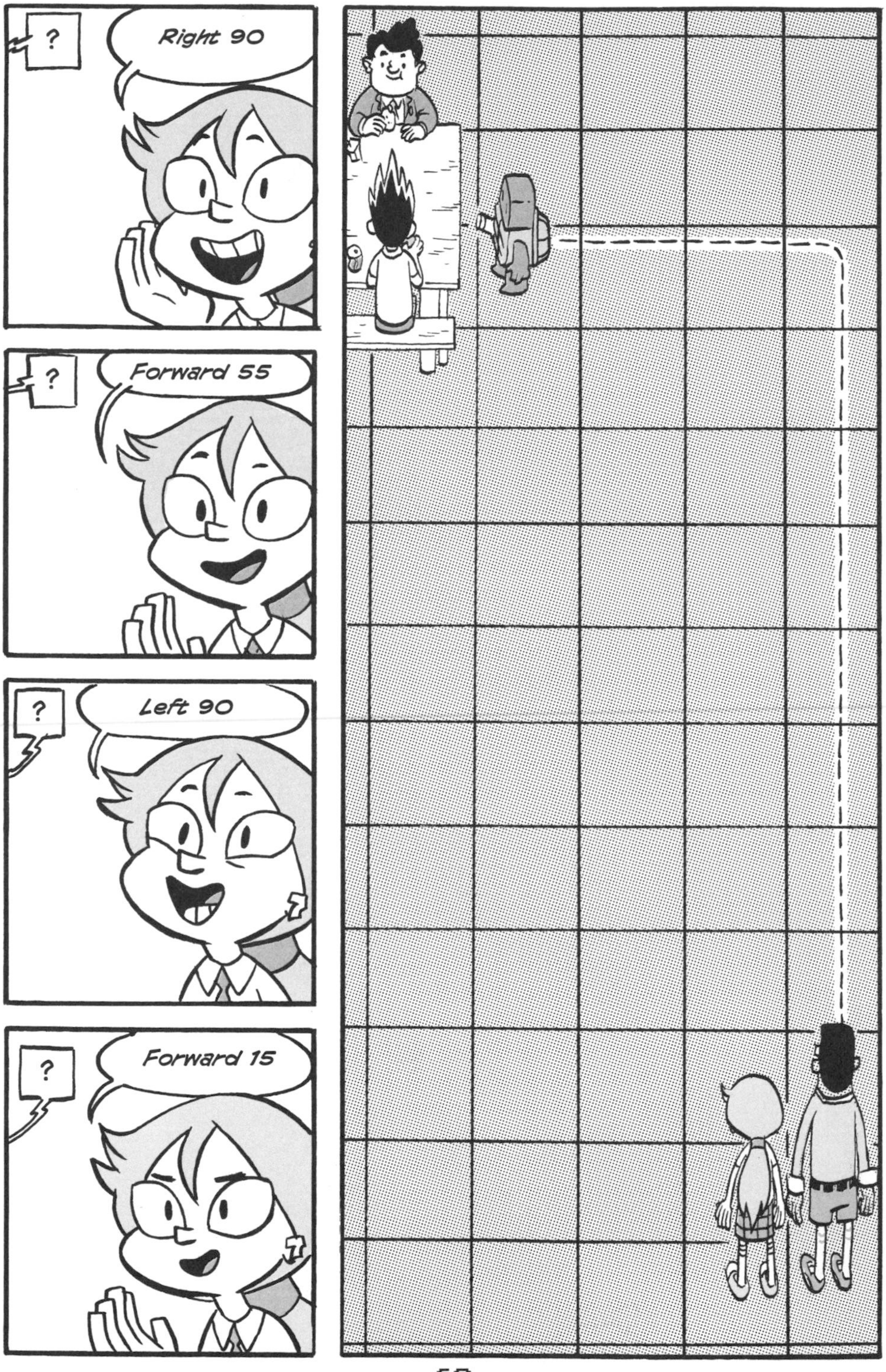
?
Right 90
?
Forward 55
?
Left 90
?
Forward 15

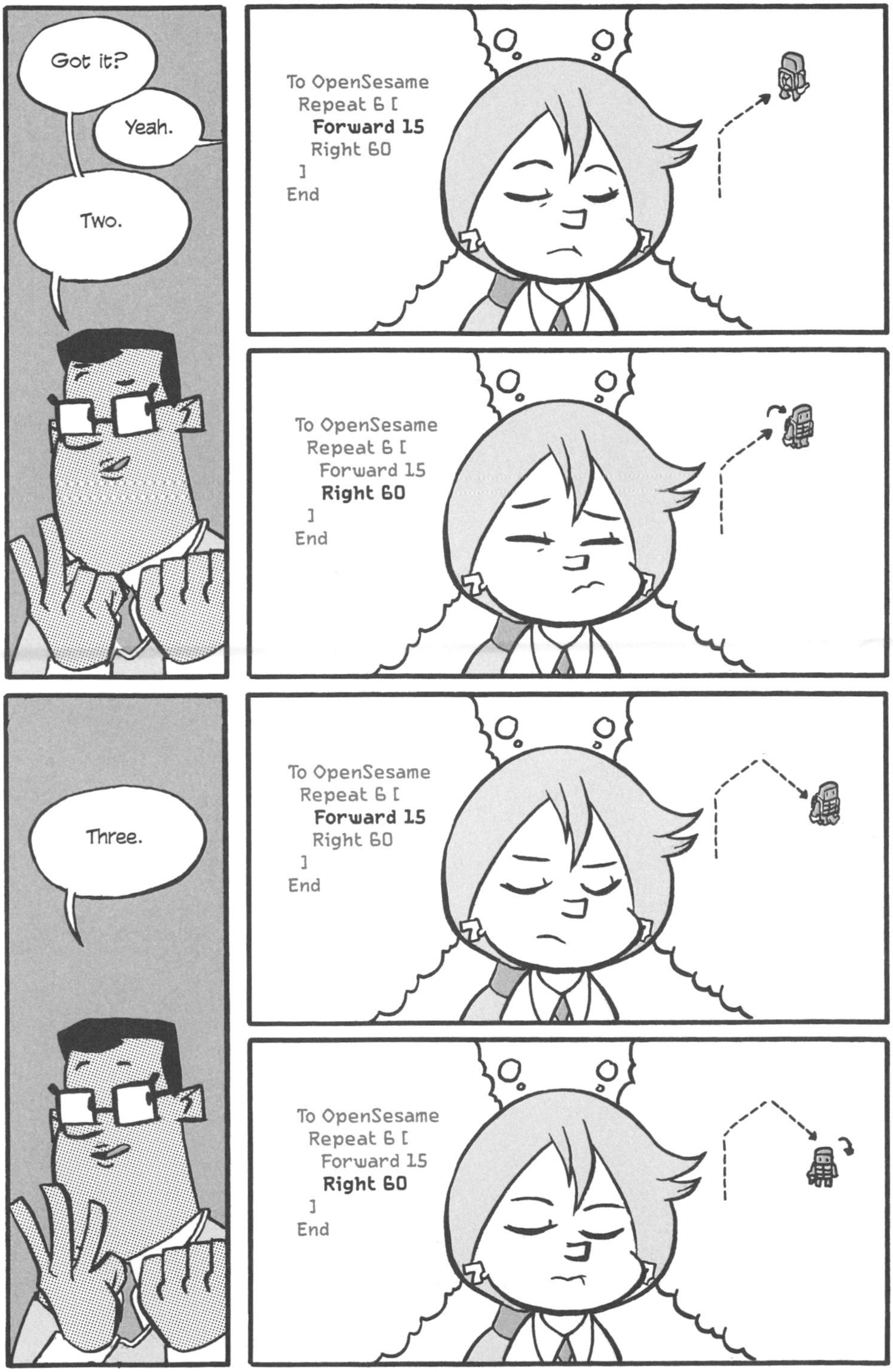
Got it?
Yeah.
Two.
To OpenSesame
Repeat 6 [
Forward 15
Right 60
]
End
To OpenSesame
Repeat 6 [
Forward 15
Right 60
]
End
Three.
To OpenSesame
Repeat 6 [
Forward 15
Right 60
]
End
To OpenSesame
Repeat 6 [
Forward 15
Right 60
]
End

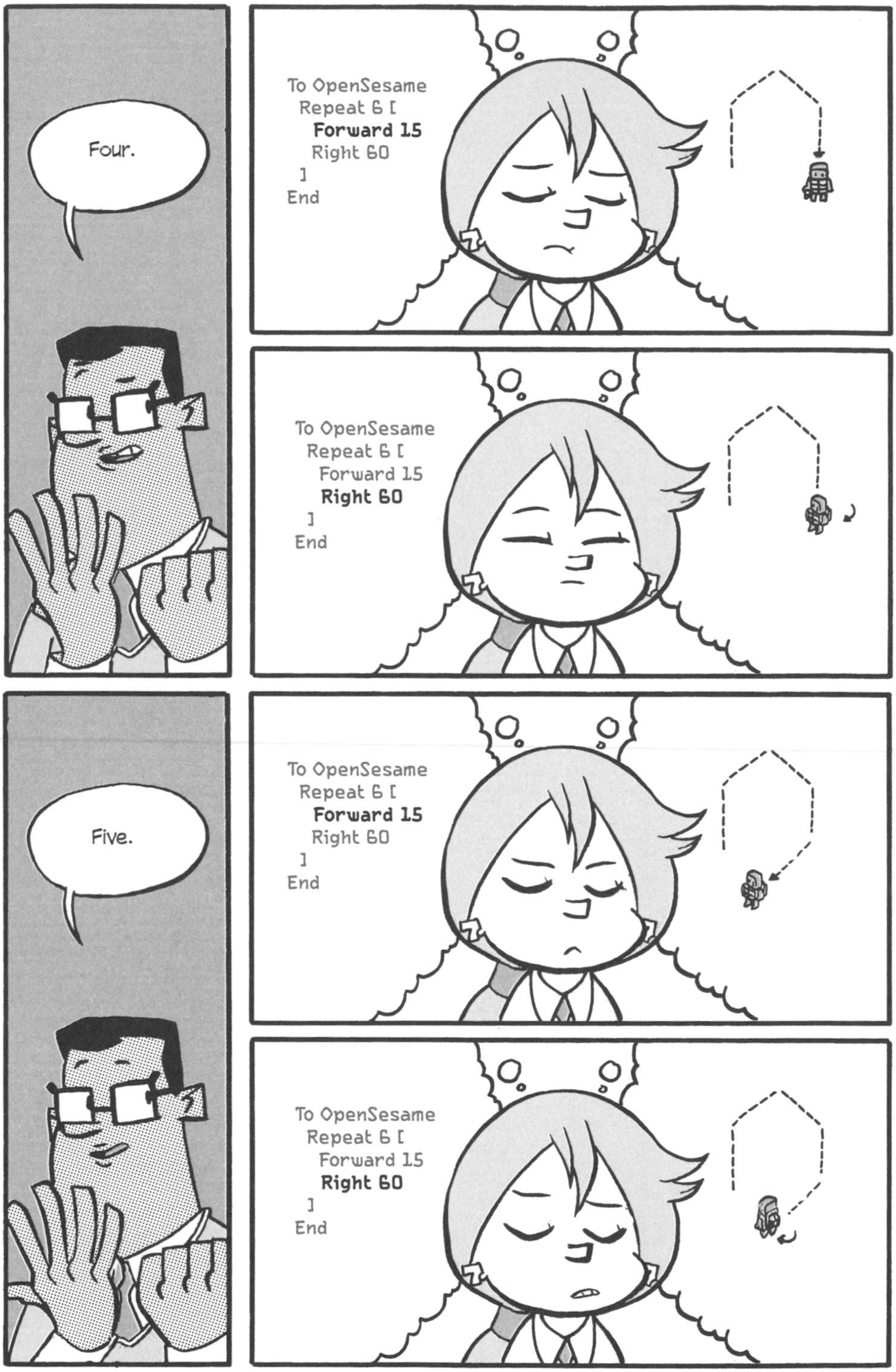
Four.
To OpenSesame
Repeat 6 [
Forward 15
Right 60
]
End
To OpenSesame
Repeat 6 [
Forward 15
Right 60
]
End
Five.
To OpenSesame
Repeat 6 [
Forward 15
Right 60
]
End
To OpenSesame
Repeat 6 [
Forward 15
Right 60
]
End

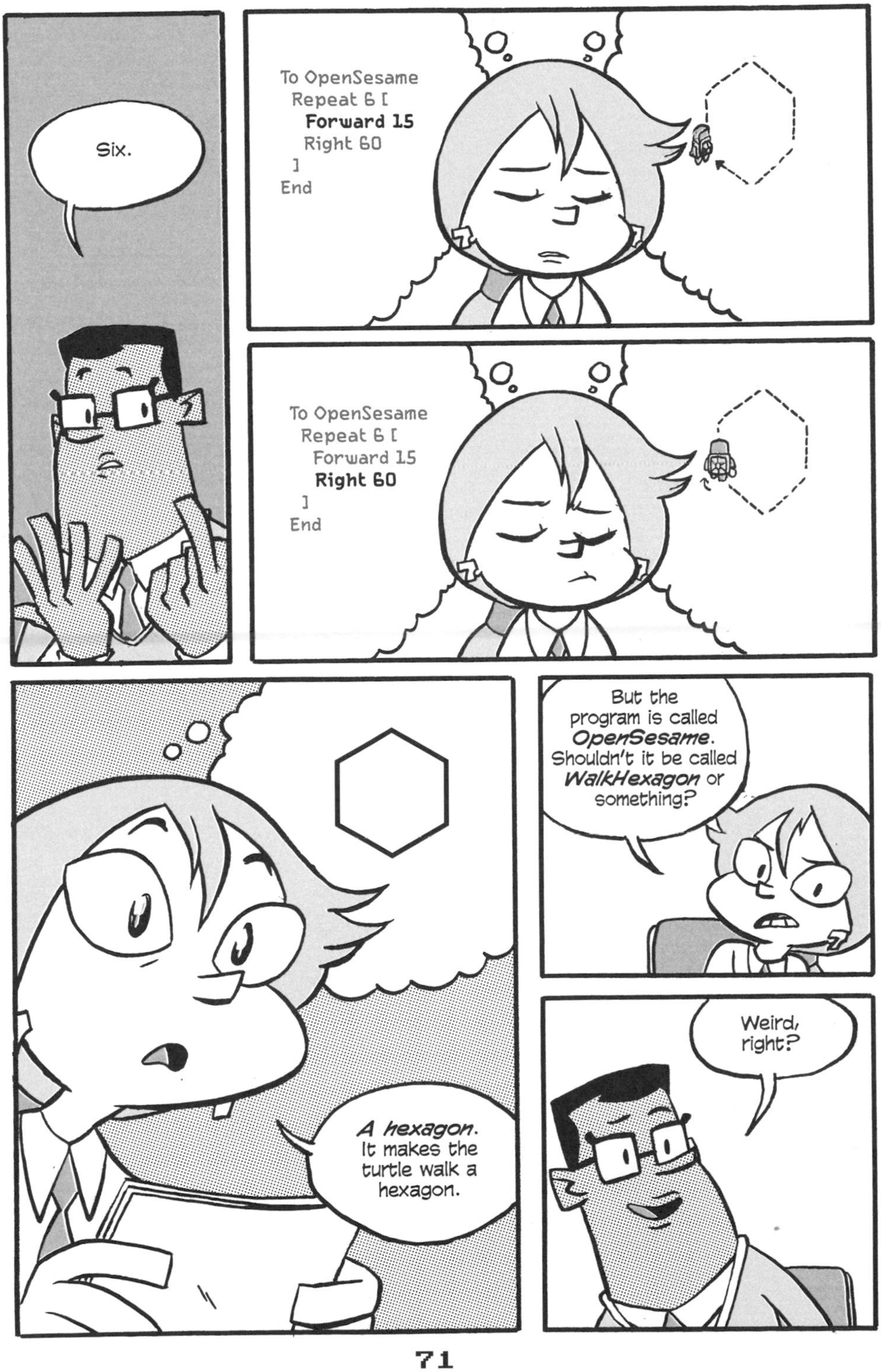
Six.
To OpenSesame
Repeat 6 [
Forward 15
Right 60
]
End
To OpenSesame
Repeat 6 [
Forward 15
Right 60
]
End
A hexagon. It makes the turtle walk a hexagon.
But the program is called OpenSesame. Shouldn't it be called WalkHexagon or something?
Weird, right?

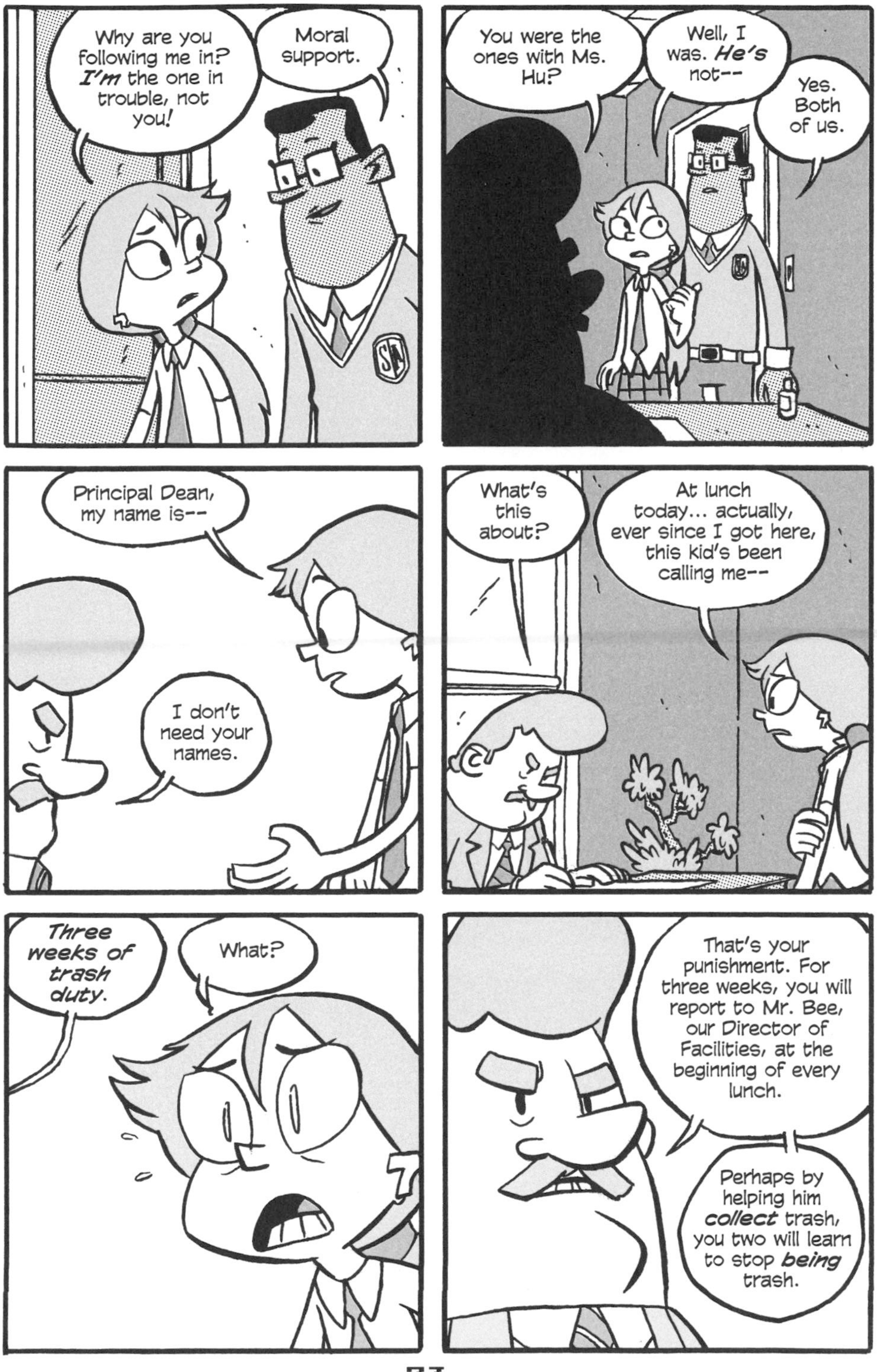
Why are you following me in? *I'm* the one in trouble, not you!
Moral support.
You were the ones with Ms. Hu?
Well, I was. *He's* not--
Yes. Both of us.
Principal Dean, my name is--
I don't need your names.
What's this about?
At lunch today... actually, ever since I got here, this kid's been calling me--
Three weeks of trash duty.
What?
That's your punishment. For three weeks, you will report to Mr. Bee, our Director of Facilities, at the beginning of every lunch.
Perhaps by helping him *collect* trash, you two will learn to stop *being* trash.

75

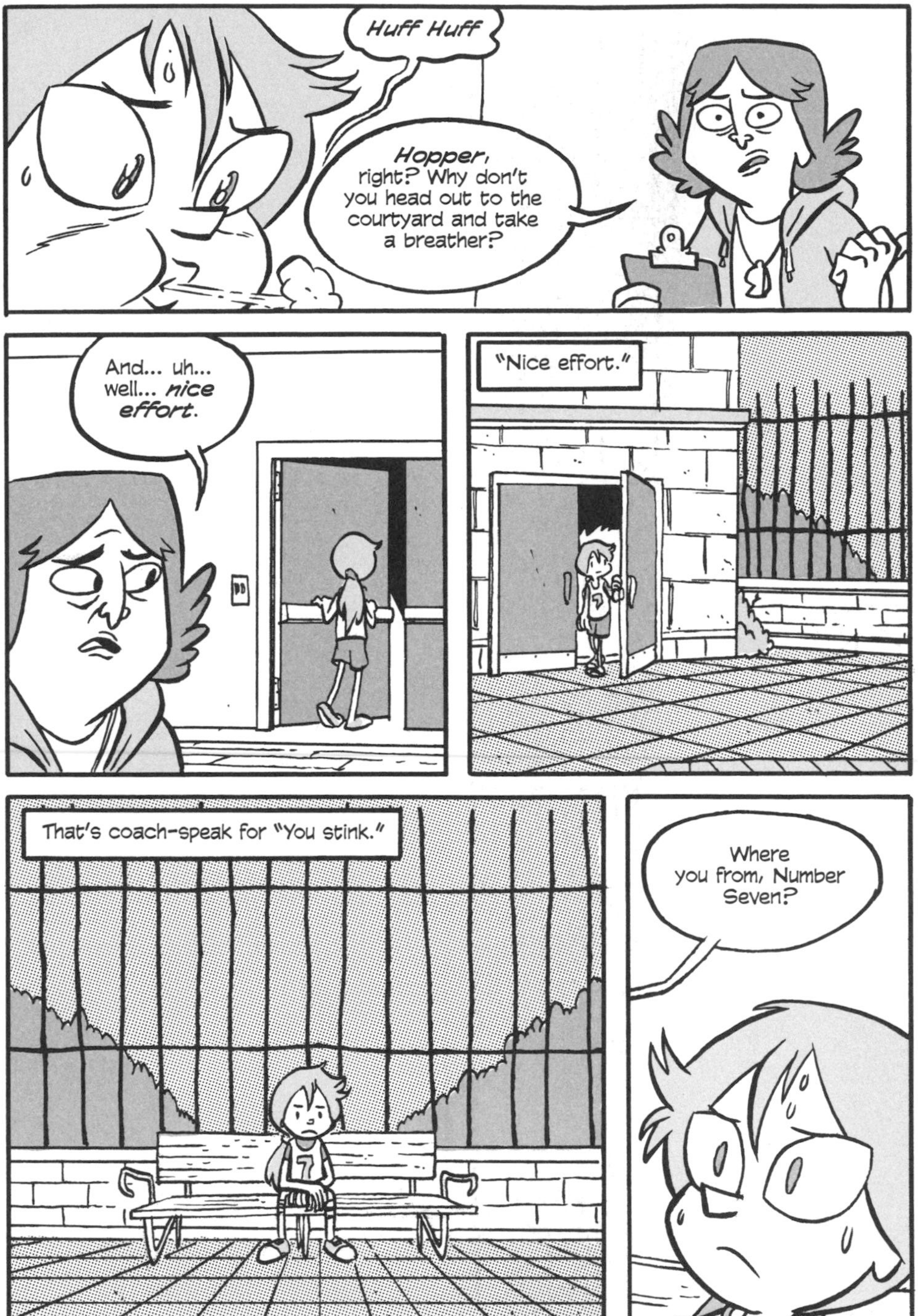
Huff Huff
Hopper, right? Why don't you head out to the courtyard and take a breather?
And... uh... well... nice effort.
"Nice effort."
That's coach-speak for "You stink."
Where you from, Number Seven?

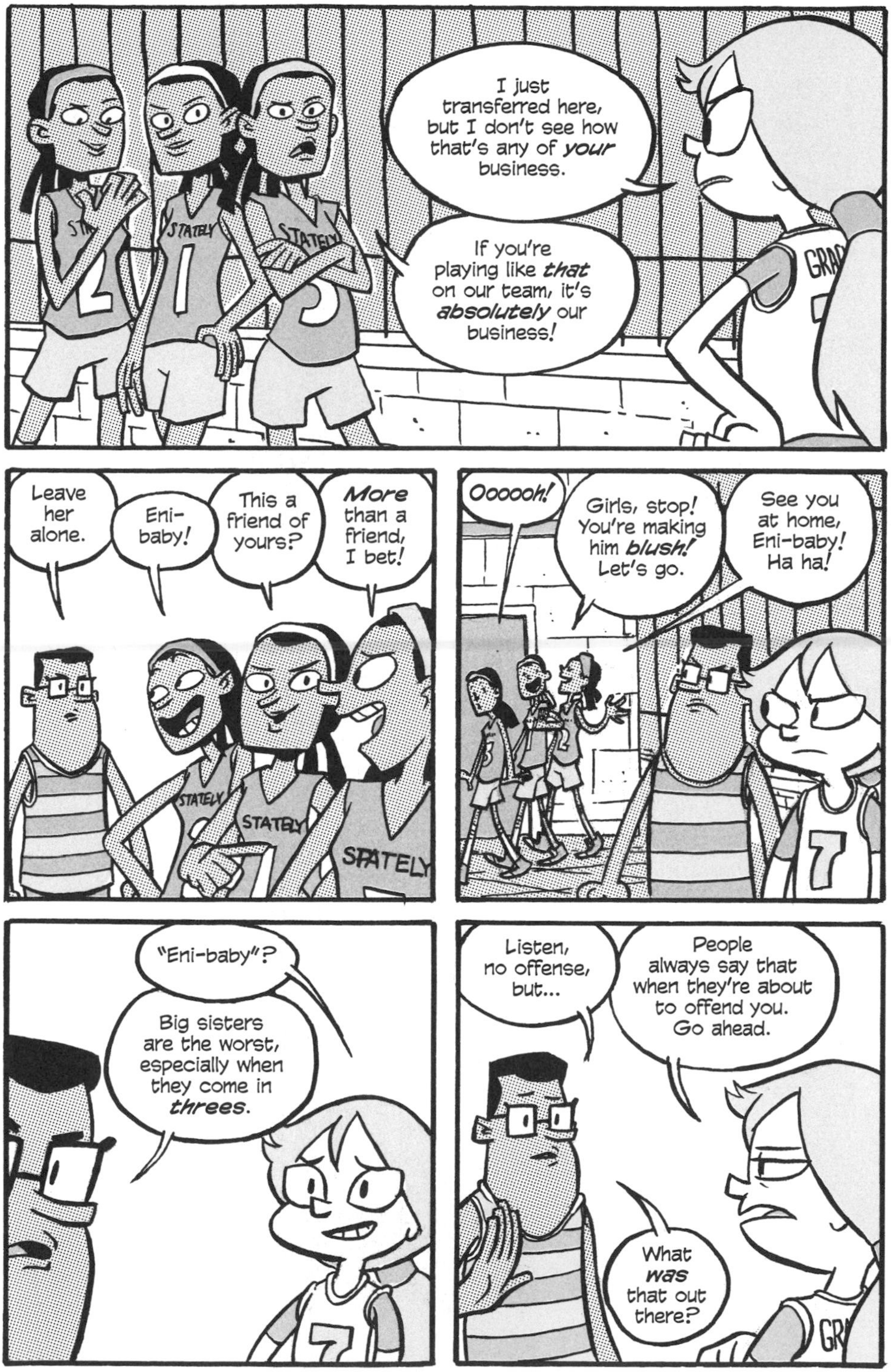
I just transferred here, but I don't see how that's any of *your* business.
If you're playing like *that* on our team, it's *absolutely* our business!
Leave her alone.
Eni-baby!
This a friend of yours?
More than a friend, I bet!
Ooooooh!
Girls, stop! You're making him *blush!* Let's go.
See you at home, Eni-baby! Ha ha!
"Eni-baby"?
Big sisters are the worst, especially when they come in *threes*.
Listen, no offense, but...
People always say that when they're about to offend you. Go ahead.
What *was* that out there?

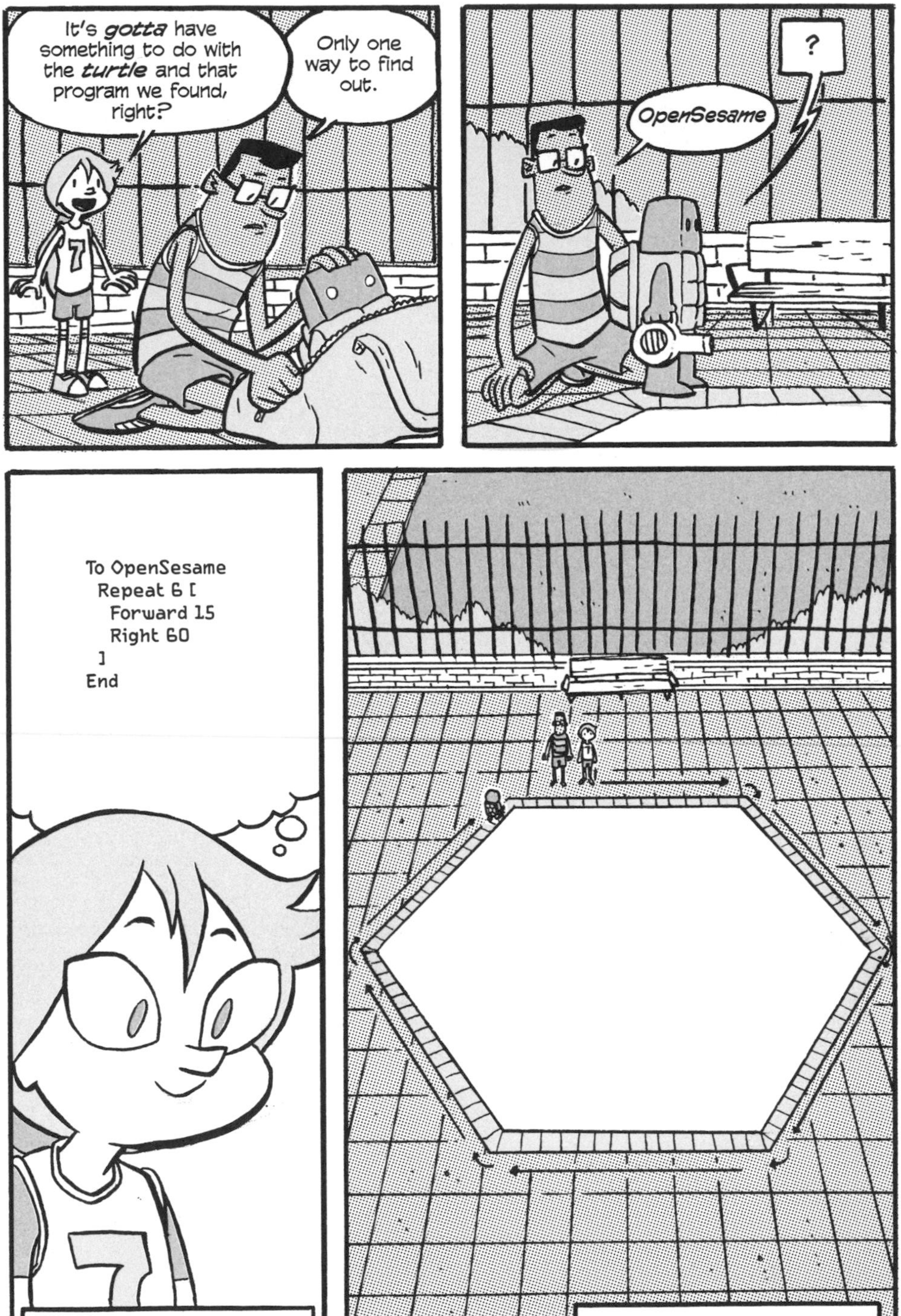
It's *gotta* have something to do with the *turtle* and that program we found, right?
Only one way to find out.
OpenSesame
?
To OpenSesame
Repeat 6 [
Forward 15
Right 60
]
End
Little guy walked a *hexagon*--
--just like how I'd *imagined*.

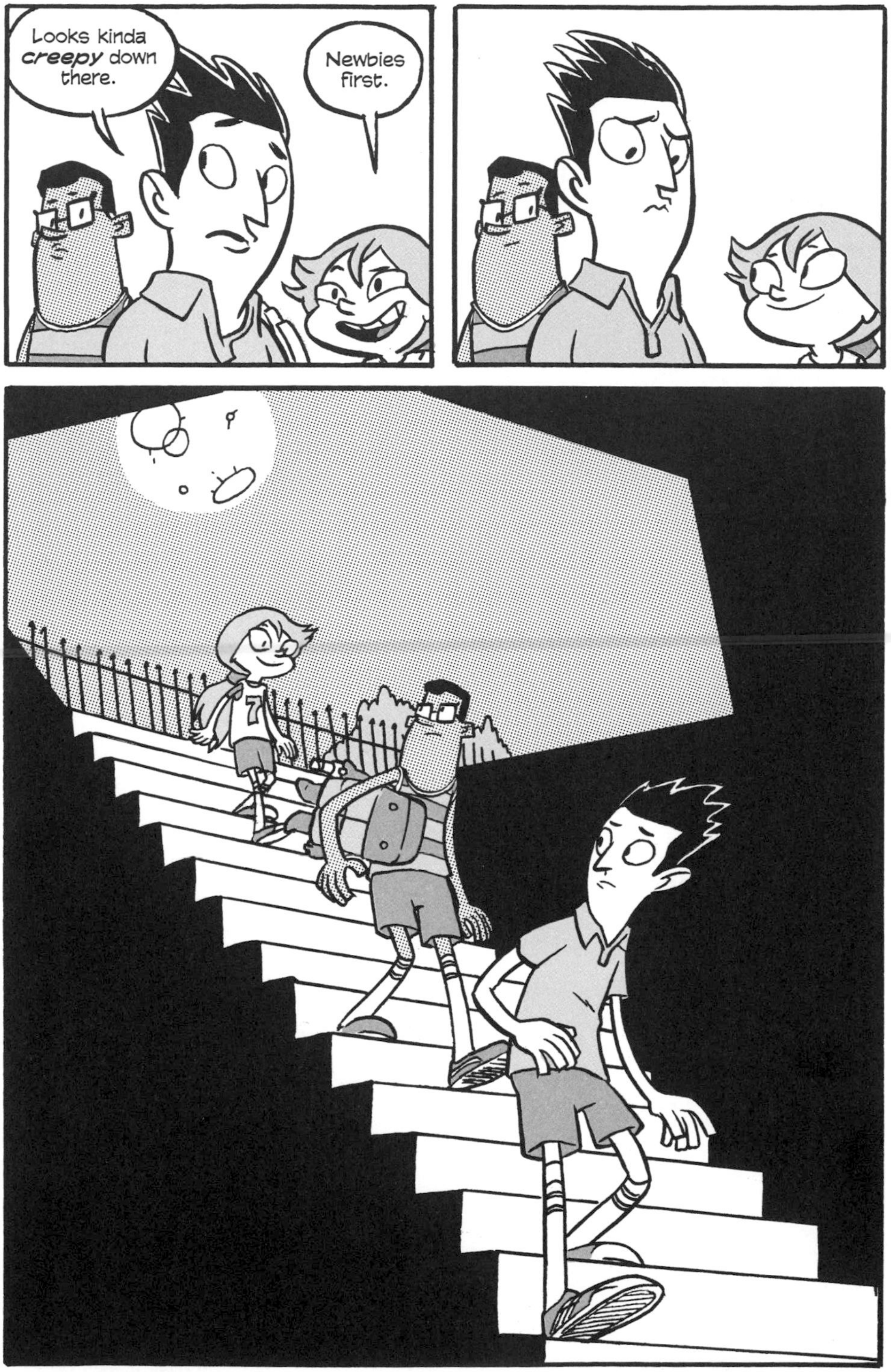
Looks kinda *creepy* down there.
Newbies first.

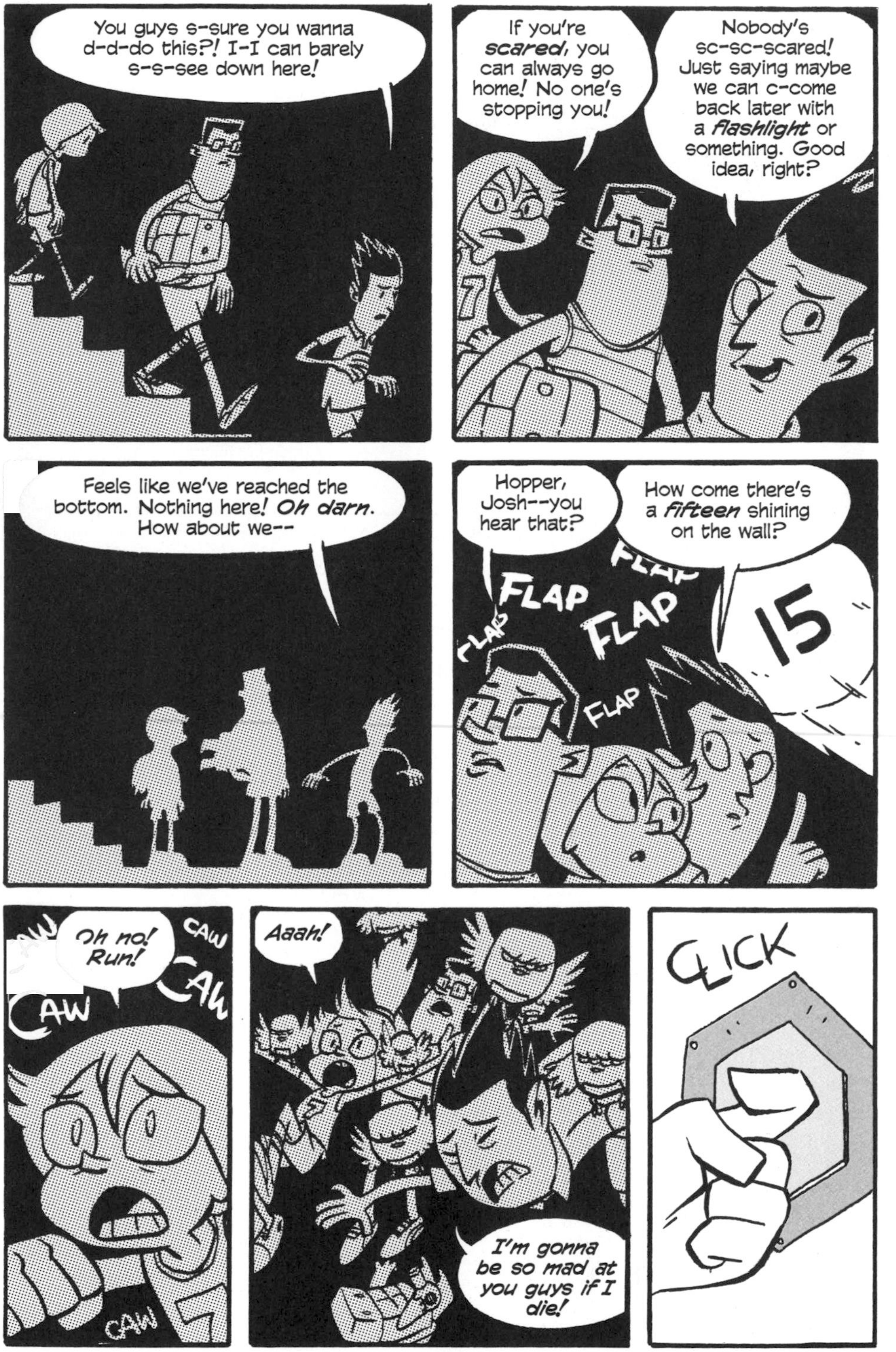
You guys s-sure you wanna d-d-do this?! I-I can barely s-s-see down here!
If you're *scared*, you can always go home! No one's stopping you!
Nobody's sc-sc-scared! Just saying maybe we can c-come back later with a *flashlight* or something. Good idea, right?
Feels like we've reached the bottom. Nothing here! *Oh darn*. How about we--
Hopper, Josh--you hear that?
How come there's a *fifteen* shining on the wall?
FLAP
FLAP
FLAP
FLAP
FLAP
15
Oh no! Run!
CAW
CAW
CAW
CAW
Aaah!
I'm gonna be so mad at you guys if I die!
CLICK

85

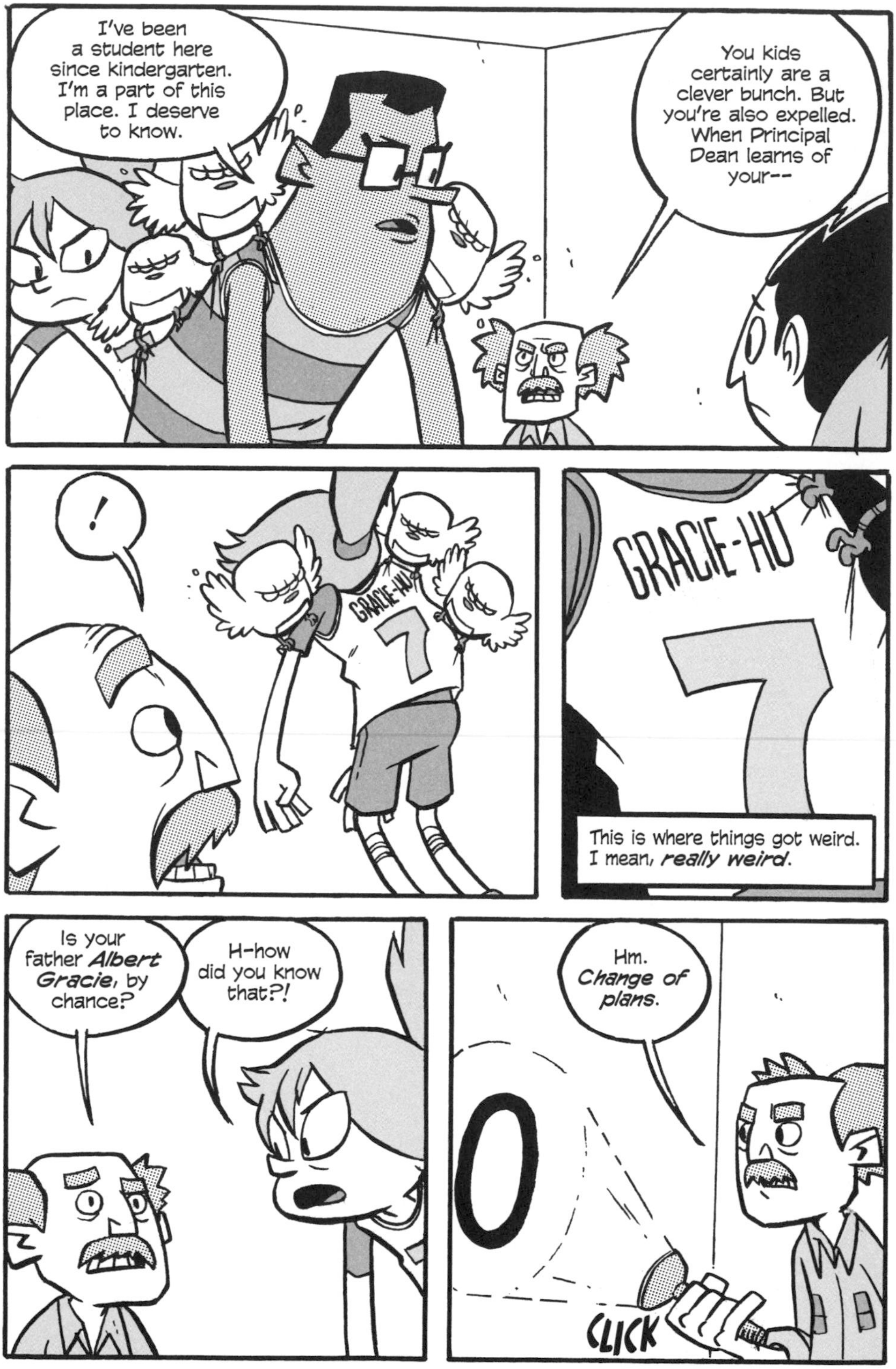
I've been a student here since kindergarten. I'm a part of this place. I deserve to know.
You kids certainly are a clever bunch. But you're also expelled. When Principal Dean learns of your--
!
GRACIE-HU
7
GRACIE-HU
7
This is where things got weird. I mean, *really weird*.
Is your father *Albert Gracie*, by chance?
H-how did you know that?!
Hm. *Change of plans*.
CLICK

Continued in

Paths & Portals

Ready to start coding?

Visit www.secret-coders.com

Check out these other books
in the Secret Coders series!

**Paths & Portals
Secrets & Sequences
Robots & Repeats
Potions & Parameters
Monsters & Modules**

Author's Note

It was the summer of 1984, and I'd just finished the fifth grade.

Everybody knows that summers are meant to be fun. You're supposed to goof off at the local swimming pool, or stage epic action figure battles, or watch endless reruns of *Voltron*. You're supposed do whatever you want as long as it doesn't involve school. After all, summer and school are opposites. Not just opposites, mortal enemies. Everybody knows that.

Unfortunately for me, my mom was not "everybody." After two weeks of *Voltron* reruns, she sent me to summer school. I had to take three, maybe four, "enrichment" classes. Now, thirty years later, I only remember one of them: Introduction to Computer Programming.

Our classroom had row after row of computers, more than I'd ever seen in one place. Computers back then weren't what they are today. The only color they displayed was green. They couldn't get on the World Wide Web because it hadn't been invented yet. They stored all their data on these flimsy black disks, and when you stuck a disk into a computer, the sound it made was a cross between a wheeze and a burp.

Even so, computers were magic.

The teacher paired me up with a kid named Bill who was a year older and a head taller. He had this weird habit of cracking his knuckles whenever he was thinking. It was annoying at first, but pretty soon I didn't mind. You see, Bill had coded before. He knew what he was doing.

Even before our first lesson, Bill could make the computer do the most remarkable things. He made it solve math problems, play music, tell jokes. And, most impressive to me at the time, he made it draw.

With just a few commands, Bill could make something intricate and wondrous appear on the screen, something resembling a burst of fireworks, or maybe an alien snowflake. Bill was a magician. I wanted to be one too.

And by the last day of class, I was. I'd learned a few simple commands that could be combined in an infinite number of ways, to accomplish an infinite number of tasks. My parents bought a computer for our family, and I didn't watch another episode of *Voltron* for the rest of that summer.

Coding is creative and powerful. It's how words turn into image and action. It truly is magic. Mike Holmes and I made the book you now hold in your hands because we want to share a bit of that magic with you, and maybe inspire you to become a magician—a coder—yourself.

Happy Coding!

Gene Luen Yang

GREAT GRAPHIC NOVELS
From the *New York Times*–Bestselling Author
Gene Luen Yang

978-1-59643-152-2

"Gene Luen Yang has created that rare article: a youthful tale with something new to say about American youth."
—*The New York Times*

BOXERS

978-1-59643-359-5

SAINTS

978-1-59643-689-3

"Read this, and come away shaking."
—Gary Schmidt, Newbery Honor–winning author

"A masterful work of historical fiction."
—Dave Eggers, author of
A Heartbreaking Work of Staggering Genius

THE EXCITING NEW SERIES

978-1-62672-075-6

"Brings computer coding to life."
—*Entertainment Weekly*

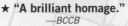

978-1-59643-697-8

★ "A brilliant homage."
—BCCB

978-1-59643-235-2

"Bravura storytelling."
—*Publishers Weekly*

THE ETERNAL SMILE

978-1-59643-156-0

★ "Absolutely not to be missed."
—*Booklist*

:01
First Second
NEW YORK